THE ACCIDENTAL MOVIE STAR

EMILY EVANS

For upcoming books and other information, visit www.EmilyEvansBooks.com.

[1. Fiction. 2. Romance. 3. Young Adult.]

Formatted by IRONHORSE Formatting

ISBN: 1477582312
ISBN-13: 978-1477582312

ACKNOWLEDGMENTS

Thanks! You're awesome: Michelle, Teresa, Veronica, Jennifer, Stacy, Joellen, Barbie, Brennan, Joseph, Megan, Mishann, Rachel, Wayne, Darlene, Jeff, Heather, Trevor, Mom & Dad.

CHAPTER 1

Dad didn't show up.

The LAX baggage carousel kept rotating, but the tumble of arriving bags had ended about ten minutes ago. All around Ashley, passengers hugged their loved ones and headed toward the exits. Everyone paired up and moved on except her.

She should've known he'd forget. Mom had warned her. Successful people in Hollywood put work first, and Dad was successful. Her stomach twisted. She sank onto one of the seats, and kept a foot hooked around her bag so Los Angeles thieves wouldn't get any ideas.

The announcer said, "Please do not leave your baggage unattended. Unattended baggage may, and unattended belongings will, be treated as a threat to the facility."

Tired of waiting and moments from becoming a threat to the facility herself, Ashley grabbed her cell phone and dialed Dad's number. "I'm at passenger pickup. Where are you?"

A long pause. Then Dad said, "I sent a limo. I thought it'd be fun."

Ashley swallowed and stopped searching the faces of the people coming through the door. *Lie.* He'd forgotten.

"I'll call and check on the car." Dad clicked off.

Smack. The sound came from the glass wall beside her ear and she turned to look outside. Pink fingernails lay curled against the glass. A second hand joined the first and teenage eyes peered in. Creepy. Ashley jumped up, clutching her warm phone. Time to move on.

The peeper belonged to a member of the crowd growing outside baggage claim. Every minute Ashley had waited, at least ten more people showed up, most of them tweens accompanied by their moms. They held cameras, handmade signs, and an eagerness that foretold the arrival of a major star. Why hadn't Dad picked her up like he said he would?

Her cell phone beeped. Ashley checked the screen. The incoming text message read, *Black limo at passenger pickup, main exit.*

Now the challenge would begin. People around her had taken one look at the crowd and used alternative exits. Ashley didn't have that luxury. She grabbed the black handle of her roller bag and stepped through the glass doors labeled *Private Cars*. The dry air hit her, so different from Houston, and she breathed in exhaust and the cooler temperatures that marked LA.

After two feet, Ashley couldn't go forward. Four tweens wearing identical T-shirts and mango-scented perfume obstructed her path. She moved left. They moved left. She moved right. They moved right. Each one blocked better than the Houston Texans had all last season. The giggling fan girls who lacked any sense of personal space moved closer to the door, forcing her back a step. One of their handmade sign poked at her right arm. Ashley moved left and got a jab to the ribs. There was no way back.

The pale one directly in front of her stilled, but only for a second, then she went wild with activity. Her camera flew up, and she bounced up and down in her lime-green shoes. She led the surge toward the building. The girls rushed forward, their gloss-covered lips open in ecstatic screams, exposing multicolored braces to the world.

The tweens must have spotted their prey. A camera flashed in her face. Perfume-coated oxygen filled her lungs and she flinched as the taller one screamed right by her ear. Deafened, blinded, and rapidly losing her sense of smell, Ashley raised her driver's license and waved in the direction of the street. A man jerked her bag away. Ashley hoped he was the driver and not an LA scam artist, but at this point she didn't care either way.

She trailed the roller bag, trying not to lose sight of it in the crush. It rolled toward the street, knocked against the knees of a guy in skinny jeans and scraped a girl in Capri pants. Caught up in their frenzy, the fans didn't seem to notice the pain. They also ignored Ashley's "Sorry" and "Pardon me." Her bag paused for a moment beside the black door of a limo. The man opened it for her and moved past, carrying her bag to the trunk.

A limo. She'd gotten worse apologies from Dad. Ashley threw herself in. She landed on soft gray leather and stretched to shut the door behind her, muting the yells. A pleasant new car smell replaced the smell of conflicting perfumes. Ashley dropped her backpack and crawled to her knees to peer out the rear window. Wide, young eyes, set in flushed faces, stared back at her through the glass.

These are my peers.

The stares shifted, focusing on a guy outside her limo. He wore dark sunglasses and jeans. A teal T-shirt stretched tight across his chest and biceps. No doubt he'd had the fabric tailored to show off that physique. Two burly men in dark suits flanked him. Their bulk made his lean swimmer's body stand out even more. Nice.

The limo door opened, and feminine shouts of "I want to have your baby" and "Caspian" and "I love you" floated in.

As he climbed in, a hot-pink lace bra flew past his head and landed on her shoulder. Ashley flicked the underwire and the gift tumbled off her shoulder, coming to rest against the plush carpet in open hot-pink abandon. The door slammed, and late-flying bras from the slow throwers plopped against the glass and fell to the LA street.

The guy pulled his sunglasses off and dropped his head against the leather seatback. His chin-length, streaked blond hair and deep blue-green eyes were instantly recognizable.

Movie star Caspian Thaymore had just gotten into her car.

It looked like she was sharing her ride.

At the sight of Ashley, a female teenager, Caspian sighed and pasted on a practiced smile that didn't show in his eyes. Leaning toward her, he said in his rich British accent, "Here you go." He snagged her wrist, grabbed a marker from his pocket, opened it with his teeth, and scribbled across her arm. The ink pierced the new limo smell, but beneath both of those fragrances she smelled his cologne: foreign, male, unique.

After a second of the soft tip gliding over her skin, Ashley slapped the marker away. "What are you doing?"

Caspian ignored her and flipped on the intercom. "We have a passenger," he said to the driver.

The car moved away from the curb and the driver said, "She's on the list."

Caspian released the switch, giving them back their privacy.

Ashley checked out her arm. The smeared black ink read *Caspian Thaymore*. A hooked curve straggled underneath his signature, as if he'd been drawing a heart below his name before she'd knocked the marker away. Wow, that would have set the tweens to screaming, parents too. She licked her thumb and rubbed at the autograph. The ink smeared around, but stayed on her skin, his name and half a heart.

Dad worked at a major motion picture studio, so after age twelve, autographs had stopped being exciting, as had movie stars. Their heroic on-screen personas never matched the reality, so meeting them killed the illusion. Today her tolerance for spoiled men was about gone. Dad had used up the last of it, and before him, there'd been a three-hour flight in a middle seat. The men on each side of her had hogged the armrests and flapped their elbows out, not caring that they dug into her sides. Now this guy thought he needed a ten-seater limousine all to himself and wanted to use her as a canvas. "I think you're the passenger in my car." Ashley jerked a thumb toward the back window. "I bet that's your ride."

A few yards behind them, a white Hummer limousine rested against the curb, a spike-heeled brunette posed alongside it. Ashley recognized her. The actress was named Petra something. Pelinski. Petra Pelinski. Photographers, carrying enormous cameras, focused on her. Petra feigned shock by holding a hand to her mouth. Then she hooked her hips out for a few frames before stepping into the vehicle with an unnecessarily high lift of her skirt. The hike revealed a sapphire-laden garter that matched her sapphire anklet, bracelet, necklace, and earrings.

Ashley witnessed the whole scene because the limo had barely moved from the curb due to the traffic and the crowds. Hollywood. She turned back to Caspian. "I guess you can share with me," she offered with a tone of gracious generosity in her voice.

"Thanks," Caspian said, somewhat drily, in his clipped British accent. He threw a quick glance at the monstrosity that dwarfed their sleek limo. "This car's a Jaguar."

"So?"

"A Jaguar."

Ashley raised her eyebrows. Huh?

"Jaguars have British backgrounds. I bet it's my car."

They probably had sent the limo for him, and Dad threw her along for the ride. "Oh." The car crawled forward, and Ashley slouched in her seat, deciding she may as well get comfortable because at two miles per hour, the ride to Burbank would take a while. "I'm Ashley."

"Hi."

"I'm interning at the studio for the summer."

Caspian looked bored. "I'm Caspian Thaymore."

"I guessed as much from the screams."

"Call me Caz."

Ashley slid down the bench seat and opened the minibar. "Want something?"

Caz leaned forward, elbows on the knees of his dark trousers. "Yes, please. A beer."

Ashley tossed him a cold bottle of orange juice. California had the best OJ in the world, after all. He should be thankful. "Nice try. You're not twenty-one. The drinking age is twenty-one in the US." She didn't care if he drank a beer, but he deserved payback over the autograph. She took a beer to annoy him, and used the edge of her T-shirt to twist off the silver cap.

"You're not twenty-one either." Caz read aloud the logo painted across her Texas high school T-shirt: "Trallwyn High Seniors Rule." The words sounded funny in his accent.

Ashley straightened the hem of her favorite shirt, the one her best friends Marissa, Michelle, and Steve had signed, and she took a drink from the brown bottle. It tasted bitter and sour, and smelled worse. Poor choice. "Yuck."

Caz took the bottle from her hand. He drank a swig then pressed the clear bottle of OJ into her palm. Whatever. She preferred juice anyway.

The car picked up speed. Ashley looked at the passing palm trees and rock-laden landscapes. They were going at least thirty miles per hour. In LA, that was practically a high-speed chase. *Goodbye, LAX. See you in three months.* Ashley tapped his bottle with hers, making the glass thump. "Cheers."

"Cheers." Caz repeated the toast automatically. It was an ingrained reflex for the British.

The limo jerked to the right and the force of the motion propelled her across his lap and him against the wall. She dropped the juice and clutched his arm, trying to stay upright. The bottle rolled across the floorboard, emptying its pulpy orange contents into the plush weave of the carpet.

"Sorry." Ashley tried to grab the back of the seat, but the car swerved again and her fingers slid across the leather without success. She gave in and grabbed Caz's shoulder to pull herself upright. He helped with one arm, while retaining a grip on his beer bottle with the other.

The car jerked. Beer sloshed. Then, with a sudden burst of speed, the Jaguar slid sideways, flinging them from side to side like they were on a Tilt-A-Whirl. With a final tire squeal, the Jaguar jolted to a stop.

They tumbled to the floor and Ashley found herself sprawled across Caz, face-to-face, body-to-body.

Chapter 2

Ashley peered through the pale strands of her disheveled hair. Piercing blue green eyes met hers. She broke the gaze and focused the empty beer bottle rolling on the floor above his head. The bottle didn't stop until the base butted up against the hot-pink bra.

The limo door opened and a bright flash went off. Automatically, Ashley turned away. Another flash went off. Crawling backwards, she eased off Caz. He cursed as he sat up, and his hair flopped into his eyes. He looked like a bad-tempered fallen angel, impossibly beautiful. If the photographer got that shot, he'd make a mint.

From outside the car, the driver yelled, "Hey, you," and shut the door, ending the impromptu photo shoot.

"You okay?" Caz's voice sounded more clipped than before.

"Yeah." Ashley got to her knees. "You?"

"Yeah."

Ashley examined her beer-spattered T-shirt and jeans with regret. She couldn't see the back of her shirt, but the stickiness of the drying orange juice assured her it was a mess. When the limo shifted forward, she grabbed the side of the seat and pulled back into it. She patted the wall until she found the seatbelt and secured it low and tight across her lap, like the airlines recommended. *Click.* Caz put his on too.

The intercom came on and the driver said, "The press is getting out of hand, I had to swerve to avoid them. You two okay back there?"

Caz didn't look ruffled, and his clothes weren't as wet as hers. Ashley watched his reaction with caution, bracing for the tears, the rage, the threat of lawsuits, and the list of personal injuries he'd endured.

"We're fine," Caz said, and settled back for the ride.

"No problem," Ashley said.

The Jaguar prowled smoothly for the rest of the trip, and a short time later pulled into a private garage at the studio's lot. They had arrived.

Caspian got out first, with a "See ya," and walked over to a tall, thin woman who stood only a few yards away, puffing on a cigarette.

Just past them, Dad appeared in a doorway. She waved, grabbed her backpack by its handle, and jogged over to hug him. *Dad.*

He hugged her and slung one arm around her shoulders as he moved toward the building. Ashley noticed he wore his pale blond hair short this summer, so she could clearly see his light blue eyes narrow when he looked back at Caz and the limo. His eyes were the same shade as hers, and at the moment they held a suspicion. He must've smelled the beer. Ashley spoke quickly to head off the lecture. "The minibar exploded." She lifted the end of her long hair and gave the blond strands a sniff. "Ew, right?"

Around Dad's back, she saw Caz glancing at them. He shot a look from her to Dad. She'd seen that contemptuous expression before. At home, they'd guess father-daughter reunion, especially as they shared the same coloring. Here in LA, they always assumed older boyfriend—disgusting.

Dad's arm tightened and he held the door for her to go in. They went down a gray hallway then took one flight of stairs down to the basement level. Dad stopped at a door marked *Human Resources*. "Good luck."

Ashley swiped a hand at her shirt. "My appointment was supposed to start thirty minutes ago."

"It's not a problem," Dad said.

Ashley reached for the doorknob. Her first day on the job and she was about to make a beer-soaked impression. Luckily, she had a spare T-shirt in her bag and nepotism by her side.

***

Ashley's second day on the job started out cleaner. She drove one of Dad's cars and parked in the employee lot. Dad worked in one of the stucco executive buildings along the front. She'd thought they'd commute together, but Dad said last night that his hours were too erratic, so here she was walking in alone. The warm air brushed against her skin, the dry climate amazing. If California could bottle their weather and sell it to the humid states, their budget crisis would be over.

Ashley breathed in and looked around. She'd seen most of the movie studio as a tourist on summer visits. Now she was seeing the lot with fresh employee eyes. Grassy parks came before the façades of fake towns. After those, there was a sea of concrete and a multitude of warehouses that held the movie sets.

She checked the signs carefully for warehouse number 47. The buildings appeared the same to her: tin metal squares placed atop acres of concrete pavement. She thought it was odd for creative people to work in such bland buildings. Ah, there it was, number 47, her set for the next few months.

A security guard perched on a stool by the narrow doorway, opaque sunglasses shielding his eyes. He said, “Identification,” in a voice that implied she couldn’t provide a legitimate one.

Ashley showed him her driver’s license and her studio identification card. The guard shined a light on the back of the card, examined her face, and checked his clipboard. “You’re good.” He waved her on. “The kickoff meeting is inside.”

Inside, people milled near two long folding tables or lined up to speak with a pointy-faced man holding a computer tablet. Ashley dropped into line.

The man scanned the screen while he stroked his goatee. “Production Assistant?”

Ashley nodded.

“I’m the assistant director. Call me AD.” He paused, so Ashley nodded again. At her nod, he grunted and said, “Run this script over to Petra’s trailer.”

Yesterday, Ashley had received a small movie summary from Human Resources and knew that Petra Pelinski was the lead actress who was playing the part of a spy vixen. Even more interestingly, Caspian Thaymore would play opposite her as the tortured hero. She’d buy a ticket. Ashley took the clipped stack of red pages from the AD and left the line. Security must be tight around this film if they were printing scripts on red. Red paper couldn’t be photocopied.

“Trailer six,” the AD called after her and jerked his hand toward the rear of the warehouse. Ashley went in that direction.

Another security guard blocked the back exit. Ashley showed her identification and told him her task. The guard pointed beyond the building. A number of white trailers were parked along back, each labeled with a large black number. The quiet calm behind the building was a distinct contrast to the loud frenzy occurring steps away. The crunch of gravel under her sneakers echoed each step to trailer number six.

She tapped on the door. No answer.

Tap, tap, tap.

No response and no mail slot. Not wanting to fail her first assignment, Ashley turned the knob. The door opened easily and she leaned in. A red leather sofa sat in a compact living room underneath a long horizontal picture of Petra. Bingo. She was at the right trailer. A gust of heavy Asian perfume blew out. Her nose twitched and she stuck her hand underneath it. She breathed in the neutral smell of paper and tried not to sneeze.

A female voice emerged from further back in the trailer. “Like can you imagine? I’ll be on this set for at least two months.” Petra’s East Coast accent punctuated the words. “It is so much better than location shots. All the best salons are here. All the best of everything is here. Everyone knows me. I can get the right press.”

“Of course, you’ll make headlines for just being here,” a different female voice said in a barking tone. No way the barker was an actress, not with that voice. “But imagine if something exciting happened, like if you were to get pregnant—with Caspian’s baby.” The voice alternated between barking out the words and clipping them off.

“If I show up pregnant with Caspian’s baby? Why would I want that? I’d be so fat.” There was a pause, and Ashley stood very still in the doorway.

The barker said, “Imagine the press.”

“The coverage would be amazing,” Petra said. “And everyone is getting pregnant or adopting right now, so we could go maternity shopping, me and all the other big stars. I’ve worked with Caspian before, but we’ve never, you know. What if he doesn’t want a kid right now? He’s only like eighteen.”

“No guy can resist you,” the barker said. “How hard is it to get preggers? Punch a hole in the condom.”

There was a longer pause, then Petra said, “Then I could lose the baby tragically, or he’s loaded so I could keep the baby. I would look stunning in maternity clothes. And my child would be such a pretty baby because Caspian and I are both so good looking, and I could dress her like me.”

Ashley’s mouth fell open. The East Coast voice got louder, as if Petra was moving toward the living room, toward her.

She jerked back and closed the door as quietly as she could. Safely outside, she banged the side of her fist loudly on the sun-warmed trailer door and yelled out in a formal voice, “Script update for Petra.” Ashley opened the door a crack, threw the red script in, and snapped the door shut. She hopped down from the steps, her tennis shoes crunched into the gravel, and she took off. Each pounding step kicked up more loose rocks. Ashley crossed her fingers, hoping she wouldn’t slip, but she didn’t slow until she reached the warehouse entrance. *Please don’t let me get caught.*

Out of breath, she held up her identification badge from the lanyard around her neck and showed it to the security guard. While he reviewed it again, being as thorough as the guy in the front, she checked back over her shoulder, ensuring there was no one in pursuit. The alley remained empty, but the door on Petra's trailer opened. Ashley flattened against the metal wall. At the guard's nod, she passed the threshold into the cavernous warehouse. More people had filed in and most had taken seats on temporary metal bleachers set against one of the walls. Ashley headed their way, eager to get lost in the crowd.

"PA." The pointy-faced AD waved another stack of papers at her, ignoring the line of people in front of him.

"Yes?"

"I need a cup of coffee."

"How do you take it?"

"Black." He pointed. "Cart's over there."

An eager voice jumped in and barked out, "I'll get your coffee."

Ashley stiffened. She recognized the voice. She examined the newcomer warily, but the barker hurried forward from the back entrance and didn't bother to look in her direction.

The AD said, "You are…?" He scanned his list of names. Some of the people in line looked annoyed at the interruption; others chatted away, more self-involved.

"Olive Oma, PA, proud to be of service." The barker held up her security badge in two hands and inclined her head. The glint in her hazel eyes was eager when she looked at the AD. When she swung toward Ashley, her expression turned competitive.

Ashley was average height and stood as tall as the AD. Olive's brunette head came to the top of the tablet in his hands. Petite with a pixie cut, Olive wore a muted-green jumpsuit with a brown leather tool belt strapped around her waist.

The AD said, "I already gave this job to her." He pointed his chin toward Ashley and eyed Olive's tool belt. "They're having some trouble with stage B's mobile toilet. Go give 'em a hand."

"Absolutely," Olive said. "I wanted to help with the set." Olive glared at Ashley and stomped off, swinging one hand to propel her small body faster. Her other hand squeezed the handle of the wrench locked into her tool belt.

***

Ashley took a seat on the temporary bleachers. In the short time since her arrival, the space had filled like a movie theater on Friday night. Her soon-to-be co-workers spoke loudly, and several people hugged as if seeing old friends. Most dressed casually like Ashley: jeans, T-shirts, and tennis shoes. A few dressed well, and they stood out as actors or people in charge.

The AD moved toward a tall, broad-shouldered man. The man's feet were braced apart, his arms crossed over his chest, his chin raised. With that commanding air, he had to be the director or an executive. The AD imitated his stance, and the two men assessed the crowd. Ashley checked her watch. They still had about ten minutes before the scheduled start time.

A broad-shouldered guy with a buzz cut climbed up the steps, and she slid down the bench so he could get past. Ashley wished she had a friend with her. Her summer job would be much more fun if she worked with a friend. Marissa, her best friend back home, thought Ashley's LA summers were glamorous and exotic. LA teens were the same as the teens back home, with just a few more extremists; there must be some kind of drama gene bred into the community.

Before leaving Houston, she'd called Rachel, an LA friend from summers past, but Rachel was vacationing in Europe. That was probably just as well because work would suck up most of her time. She'd just need to make a friend with one of the other crew members.

An East Coast voice interrupted her thoughts. "You're in my seat," Petra said. She wore overlarge sunglasses and red lip stain. Her tone discouraged argument. Her spicy perfume discouraged breathing.

Ashley froze, recognizing the voice of the lead actress, the pregnancy plotter. She kept her eyes on the floor and slid down the cold, metal bleacher, hoping Petra hadn't seen her back at the trailer. The first girl she'd seen who was her age, and Ashley already knew they wouldn't be friends.

"You see, this row of seats is for the cast." Petra continued hammering in her point, as if Ashley hadn't already scooted down. "I'm a member of the cast. I'm a lead, actually, so don't be surprised if they call me up front. People need to see me, so I'll sit here. Otherwise, they would all try to look and see where I am." Petra twisted her glossy dark hair and snapped a stray piece into an amber-jeweled clip.

Ashley nodded, and climbed up one level on the bleachers. The steps creaked with the motion. That was a movie studio for you. Everything was constructed out of lightweight, cheap material.

Wearing jeans and a gray pullover, Caz stepped into Petra's aisle.

Oh cool. She already knew someone, a hot someone. Ashley waved. Caz showed no reaction and Ashley felt her face flush at his failure to notice her. His eyes were on the lead actress.

"Petra," Caz said and joined her. Together, they looked like the front page of a fashion magazine, one that didn't require airbrushing.

"I got here early to hold a seat for you. I've been waiting ages. You're going to owe me." Petra straightened her perfect posture by putting her hands on her lower back and arching. "I'd have thought they'd put cushions out. On my last set, we had cushioned seats. These are cold. Sometimes my costumes are thin; I can't sit on seats like this for too long."

Caz listened until a large guy wearing a kilt strolled into the building and headed their way. Even with his attention focused on the newcomer, Petra kept talking. "Cushioned seats are the only way to go. My costumes crushed less. In fact, maybe we could arrange to have them delivered. I'll let them know you and I both want cushions so the purchase shouldn't be a problem. What color do you want?"

Caz scooted down a bit, away from Petra. Before he could state his color choice, Petra said, "I'm a winter, so I look best in cool tones. I'm thinking we should get burgundy ones or maybe cerulean."

Kilt guy's long strides carried him easily across the floor, and he and Caz greeted each other with a manly shoulder slap. They spoke for a moment then were interrupted by Petra clearing her throat.

"You know Garrett, right?" Caz asked.

"I love garnets," Petra said. "Just kidding, I like all stones, not only the red ones. When I wear—"

"Garrett, not garnet," the guy corrected in a heavy Scottish accent. The Scot swiveled his gaze around the crowd and said, "Oh, there's a cute one, then." He walked along the front until he reached the empty aisle seat beside a tall blonde lady with rock star style.

Olive trotted up next and stood in front of Petra and Caz. "Coffee for Ms. Pelinski and Mr. Thaymore." She barked the word *coffee* then drew out the *e* sound when she said the word *Pelinski.*

Caz took the cup with a "thanks" and set it by his feet.

Petra took a sip of hers. "Is this mocha frap with soy?"

Olive nodded in a knowing fashion. "I read soy's your favorite."

"Well, soy was." Petra waved a hand, making her silver bracelet slide high on her slim arm. She paused to admire the gleam in the overhead lights then said, "But soy's so last year. You know what I mean. All those third world countries are running out of soy so everyone's banning it, and I have to stay current. This year I drink orange latte with one swirl of peppermint."

"I'll get that right away for you." Olive dashed toward the coffee cart, swinging her arms, knocking into the early morning desperados, weakened by their need for caffeine, who surrounded the cart. Olive used their vulnerability and her diminutive frame to advantage and popped to the front of the group. "I'm getting coffee for Petra, so, me first."

Ashley sent a quick text to her best friend back home. "It's like the 1950s. PAs fetch coffee."

Marissa replied, "Made new mustard-mayo sauce for fries."

Ashley texted back. "Outcome?"

"Customer feedback rated recipe a seven."

"That's high."

"Not good enough."

"I want to try them."

"I'll have the dish perfected when you get home. Irina came out of the office when I was putting away the free sample tray."

Ouch. Irina, the Fry Hut's part-time manager, was also seventeen, but she relished the power that came with her title with a fervor that boded well for a career as a future army colonel or third world dictator.

"Irina made me wear the fry costume and greet customers in the parking lot."

The temperature had to be at least high nineties outside in Houston. Ashley started to type her reply, when the tall man in front of the speakers said, "I'm Russ Simmons, your director."

Ashley hit the off button on her phone. The farewell music chimed out, and she slapped a hand over the speaker, trying to look innocent.

"Welcome to your first and hopefully last crew and cast meeting until the wrap party." The large group on the bleachers, who had quieted when he spoke, gave a mild cheer.

Suck-ups.

"Most of you worked with me before, and know how I work," the director said. "I concentrate on film, and leave the day-to-day running of things to our assistant director. I'll now turn this meeting over to him."

A few people clapped. The goatee-wearing AD stepped forward and raised his hairy, pointy chin. "Please call me AD. We're not working together for the next five years. We're shooting for fifty days. In that time, while on set, you will be called by your title."

The AD stroked his goatee. "I have a backup for each one of you. If you cannot meet your commitments, we will replace you. After shooting starts, the cost is prohibitive to replace the actors, obviously, because they're on film. Putting it plainly, the cast is more important than the crew."

There were a few protest murmurs from the crowd. Garrett opened a pack of cookies and shoved one in his mouth. *Crunch.*

The AD held up his tablet and motioned toward the stars. "If a cast member needs to eat, feed him. If he needs an errand done, run it. If her hem is torn and the fabric distracts her, sew it. Fix the problem or find an assistant. Issues you can't handle come to me."

His speech made sense, but somehow seemed wrong. Especially the part where all the crap would get dumped on the assistants. *Welcome to my world for the next fifty days.* Ashley pressed her palms into the cold metal ridges of the bench seat and rolled her head, reminding herself she needed this job to help her college applications stand out.

The broad shoulder of the guy next to her bumped hers and he whispered, "If you didn't get that, I'll explain. We don't matter."

She stifled a laugh.

He ran a hand over his blond buzz cut. "I'm Boomer."

"Hi, I'm Ashley."

"Didn't you hear? I'm Boomer because I'm the boom operator."

"What's that?"

"The boom pole is a long pole that holds the microphone near the actors. I also hide other microphones around the set. And they think I can be replaced. What's a movie without sound?"

"True," Ashley said.

"Besides, look at my biceps. I'm standing in front of the directors all day showing off these bad boys. I'll make the transition from crew to cast in no time."

"Oh, you're an actor?"

Boomer gave her a pitying look. "You're in LA, babe, everyone's an actor."

The guy on her other side, a small, effeminate man with a tall tuft of brown hair, gave her a very attentive look. His flowery cologne followed his turn. "Yeah. So, who do you know? How'd you get chosen to be on set? You're quite pretty. Are you an actress?"

A little blinded by his shiny shirt and unsure which question to answer first, Ashley said, "Um, no, a student, an assistant."

"Oh." The shiny shirt guy's face twitched.

"What do you—" Ashley began.

He turned his shiny back to her and gave the person on his other side a deeply interested look.

Realizing her unimportance, Ashley turned with raised eyebrows back to Boomer. He was staring at his own biceps.

She rubbed her hands on her jean-covered thighs and rolled her shoulders. *Get ready for a long LA summer.*

Boomer spoke without looking away from his biceps. "He's Cutter."

"Cutter?"

Boomer flexed his biceps toward the shiny shirt. "You know. The costume tailor guy. As if he has a shot of getting on camera before me. Did you see my guns?"

"Uh, yeah."

The bleachers swayed, going from a solid framework one moment to metal in motion the next.

"Earthquake!" someone shouted.

CHAPTER 3

Boomer jumped from the bleachers to the ground. Cutter scrambled down the bench like a monkey, sat, and edged off the bleachers. Petra held her hands in the air and two men lifted her down like a water ballerina. Other crew members did their own version of escape. The sound of collapsing metal coupled with feminine and masculine screams as her new co-workers exercised their flair for the dramatic.

Ashley took in the action from her spot on the swaying bench. Heart racing, but unable to move, she clung to the metal seat with rigid fingers. With a slow, but unrelenting move, the metal folded in on itself. Gravity forced Ashley to release her grip and slide down the bench. She landed on the concrete, cradled in the metal V of her former seat. The hard floor and awkward angle didn't hurt as much as Caz's weight. He'd fallen against her legs, trapping her in place, six-feet-something of heavy.

"Hiya," Caz said. "Ashley, right?"

Ashley shoved at his shoulders. "Earthquake!"

Caz shifted his weight and pushed to his feet. "I don't think so. Only the bleachers moved." He offered her a hand up.

She gripped his large hand and stood on shaking legs. "Not an earthquake?"

"No earthquake."

Olive, two stagehands dressed in black, and Cutter rushed over. Olive got there first. "Mr. Thaymore, are you okay? Please, please speak to us."

The foursome grabbed his arms and pulled him clear of the wreckage. Hands dusted him off and straightened his collar.

Caz brushed away the help. "Fine, fine."

Olive announced loudly, "Caspian is fine."

"His clothes are okay and he's not wearing one of the costumes, so we're good," Cutter said.

Petra stood in a corner, re-enacting the event while a man filmed her with his cell phone.

Ashley took a deep breath, trying to calm her thudding heart.

Ignoring his helpers, Caz put a hand on one of the folded seats and offered the other to her.

***

"At least the wreck ended the meeting early," Boomer said. "I was getting bored."

Ashley stood behind him in line waiting for her turn at the infirmary. Hurt or not, everyone had to get checked out. The medics triaged important actors and staff to the front of the line. The line wound so far down the hall she couldn't see any of the actors up ahead.

Ashley put her back to the wall and slid down, folding her arms around her knees. "Do they know what happened?"

"Nope." Boomer fingered a slight tear on the edge of his sleeve. Grasping the loose fabric, he tore the sleeve short, exposing more of his bicep.

Olive reached their end of the line and handed Ashley two pieces of paper.

"Do you know what happened?"

"Of course. Those bleachers were designed to hold a few tourists, not a full film crew."

"So a weak structure? Not an earthquake?"

Olive flicked her finger against the sheets in Ashley's hand, and the paper made a crisp clicking sound. "That's your call sheet. It'll tell you where you need to be and when you need to be there."

Ashley winced. "Six a.m.?"

Olive's tone challenged as she said, "I'll be here at five." Her small frame moved down the line, handing out the rest of the forms. She didn't have far to walk.

Ashley flipped her second form over. *Release and Waiver of Liability.* Three hours, one bandaged arm, one tetanus shot, and she was free to leave.

***

When her alarm rang the next morning at an ungodly hour, Ashley crawled out of her blue sheets and took a quick shower to start her day.

The pulsing hot water helped work out the soreness in her muscles, but the heat didn't do anything for the new bruises that splotched across her skin. *Thanks, metal bleachers*. She threw a jacket over her T-shirt so Dad wouldn't worry about the bruises.

Downstairs, a note stuck to the fridge, read, *Went to the studio. Keys to Audi are on the hook by the door. Dad.*

Traffic made the short commute seem long, and she had to make one embarrassing stop by a drugstore before reaching the studio.

All she had wanted this summer was to spend some time with Dad and to list an interesting job on her college applications. She had never wanted to get involved in any work drama but she couldn't overlook intentional harm to someone; hence, the drugstore purchase newly residing in her purple messenger bag.

When she got inside the warehouse, Ashley shoved it into one of the cabinets under the makeup counter. Now she needed someone to ask her to run an errand to Caz's trailer. She'd drop off the package, and her good deed would be complete. Ashley moved along the counter, past numbered, sectioned containers of powders, gels, oils, and creams. Scooping up a stray box of tissues, she popped it into a square cutout labeled *Tissues*.

The makeup artist, busy sorting through a wheeled cart that held even more potions, lifted her head to nod in approval. "Thanks." Her short bleached rock star haircut didn't move, but her fuchsia mini dress swished around her thighs. "Call me Powder." In the mirror's reflection, Powder's face, made up with slashes of solid color, looked even more dramatic beside Ashley's pale, unmade face.

Petra walked up trailed by Olive. The actress curled into one of the chairs facing the mirrors. She held up an entertainment magazine and jabbed a red, jewel-decorated nail at the glossy cover. "I posed for so many shots. Why am I not on the cover?"

Powder rolled her eyes and added more cotton balls to a tray.

Ashley looked at Petra in surprise. Did she mean to sound so egotistical?

Olive massaged Petra's shoulders while feeding her ego. "I know. You so deserve the cover. You are the lead." Glancing at the crowd of additional suck-ups around the beautiful brunette, Ashley realized how Petra could remain oblivious—everyone smiled and nodded to her face. Not one of them called her on her ego. As Ashley moved closer, her eyes widened at the image on the magazine. The cover depicted Caz lying across a gray carpet with a hot-pink bra wrapped around a beer near his head.

Petra read the caption. "Depraved young Hollywood. Caspian arrives in LA. Only here an hour, and he's already partying like a Brit on Ibiza."

She held the photo higher as a silent Caz walked up and took a seat at the other end of the makeup table. He had compressed lips and a light frown.

Petra raised her eyebrows at him. When he failed to respond, Petra continued to read. "Blah, blah, then something about an unknown blonde companion." She held the cover to the light to get a better look at the picture.

Ashley winced. She stood near enough to recognize the back of her own head. While totally annoyed on Caz's behalf, maybe he didn't mind the coverage, but she felt grateful the article didn't identify her. Having spent summers with her divorced dad, she grew up around movie people and knew lots of them didn't want a private life. Dad attracted attention-seeing flakes. Actors were the worst.

When Ashley was little, her Dad's girlfriend had taken her to the mall. After Ashley had thrown a tantrum over leaving the toy store, the actress had walked out and left her there. The ground had shaken and toys had flown off the shelves like the actress had telekinetic powers. The whole thing had been terrifying and when Dad had found the actress talking to the press rather than looking for his kid, he hadn't dated an actress since. Good policy. *Say no to egotistical actors.*

Caz turned his chair away from Petra and looked out at the set. Powder didn't let his antisocial mood put her off. She moved in front of him and clipped his hair back with a curler clippie. Next, she dabbed at his jaw line with a spongy makeup wedge. Others gave the star and his frown a wide berth, but Powder wasn't intimidated. She waved a makeup stick at him. "This'll look great," Powder said. "Trust me."

Caz made a disbelieving sound and tilted his head out of her reach.

Ashley, feeling sorry about the embarrassing photo, slipped around to the back of his chair and whispered in his ear, "Do you want me to say something? Explain what really happened?"

Caz turned his head toward her and spoke in a normal tone. "So you can get your name in the press?"

"No," Ashley said, annoyed. "So you don't come off as a man-whore who needs to be in rehab."

His bright impossibly blue-green eyes widened, and he straightened. Powder followed him, continuing to jab the sponge at his face, and Caz snapped, "Can you give us a minute?"

Powder backed off, and Ashley gave her an apologetic look.

Olive snapped to attention and popped over to Caz's other side. "I can get you whatever you need."

Caz waved Olive away with a flick of his hand. Olive stomped back to Petra, but she kept her eyes on Ashley and Caz.

Quietly, Ashley said, "If I wanted to be in the paper, I wouldn't be the 'unidentified blonde.'"

"No one but you knew I was in that car. I was supposed to be in the Hummer."

"Like I wanted to be stuck in your paparazzi traffic," Ashley said. "You fancy foreign film guys."

Caz grabbed her elbows and pulled her forward, close enough she could smell his cologne and feel his breath when he complained in her ear. "Fancy…"

Powder came back. "Sorry, but we're going to be behind schedule if I don't get your eyeliner finished."

Ashley smirked and pulled back. "Wouldn't want to interrupt your *eye makeup*." She drawled out the last two words with her most put-upon Texas twang. Nothing mocked fancy better than a Texas drawl.

Caz released her arms, but his gaze didn't leave hers, even when Powder stepped in with the promised eyeliner. Looking over Ashley, Caz sneered. "Late night with your boyfriend? He seemed a little old to keep you out past nine."

"That was my dad in the garage, you perv." Ashley stepped toward the counter. The confrontation with Caz reminded her of her purchase. Going to the end, she scooped out her purple messenger bag. "Caz, what's your trailer number? I need to drop off a package."

Powder stepped back and unclipped his hair. The strands fell forward into his eyes. "You're good to go."

Caz threaded his hair back with one hand, nodded vaguely toward Powder, and focused on Ashley. "I locked the trailer. Give it to me now." He eyed her hand atop the messenger bag and held out his own, palm up.

Eyes widening in horror, face heating, Ashley gazed at all the people working nearby. *No way.*

"Later is fine," she said, and scurried away.

Shortly after, Ashley saw Caz act for the first time, not block, not line-read, but actually act. He was amazing, mesmerizing. Now she understood all the attention and the line of fans she'd seen at the gate this morning.

"He's really good," she said to Olive, who stood nearby, eager to jump up and kiss someone's feet the moment the director yelled, "Cut."

"I know that," Olive said sharply and moved away.

It wasn't until the end of the day that the issue of the package came up again. Caz walked straight over to Ashley and asked for it.

Her lips twisted. "What's your trailer number?"

"I don't let people in my trailer. It's my home for now. Are you going to let people walk through your home?"

"I thought you actors had an open-door policy."

Caz swung a script against his leg. "Some of us are discriminating. For instance, *you're* not invited into my trailer. So give me the package." He looked around for her bag, but she'd stashed it in the makeup area rather than carry it around all day.

"Fine. I'll hang the delivery outside your trailer. What's the number?"

Caz stretched his arms over his head, drawing her eyes to his biceps. Lean, hard, perfectly on view below the short sleeves of his T-shirt. "Come on, I'm going there now."

"So, I'm invited?"

Caz didn't respond and headed toward the exit. Ashley followed him with slow steps and a small detour by the makeup table to grab her bag.

The security guard let Caz breeze through the exit. Ashley had to show him her identification card. He checked her name, her face, and his list again before he let her trail after Caz. She walked with reluctant, crunching steps, watching him unlock the door to trailer number three.

Caz didn't stop there; he went in, leaving Ashley debating with herself. Drop the bag here, hang it on the door, or forget about this idiocy all together. The door swung open from the inside. She took a step around him and inside. The trailer's interior was small, but nice: leather sofa, flat screen television, and a tiny kitchen. Furnished with a neutral décor, pleasant but lacking personality. Except the air; the air smelled like lemon soap. "Did you clean?"

Caz ignored the question, lifted his eyebrows, and gestured at the bag.

Ashley shifted on her feet. "Is this a trailer for your breaks or do you really live here?"

Caz half sat on the armrest of the couch and rolled his broad shoulders. The fabric of his shirt tightened against his muscles. "For now, I live here, but I plan to buy a place here in the States."

"Hmm," Ashley said, delaying the drop-off. This had seemed like such a good idea this morning; now the whole thing felt weird. Her stomach twisted, and she couldn't tell if she was nervous or simply hungry. All they'd had for lunch were diet sandwiches and raw veggies. She decided to forget the package and get out. "Okay. I gotta go. I'm starving." Maybe she'd make pasta tonight. Dad liked Italian, and Alfredo sauce was quick: cream, butter, parmesan. He wouldn't have to wait long for her to prepare the meal. Or, the sauce would keep in the fridge if he couldn't make it home in time for dinner.

"The package?"

"I think they put us on a diet because we broke the bleachers," Ashley offered as a distraction and took a step back.

"No, it's because we're on film. Cameras add pounds." Caz patted his flat stomach.

He had that lean, elegant look, but he'd been heavy against her legs. Her right calf had a sizeable bruise thanks to his poundage. He must weigh more than he looked. Her head tilted to the left as she assessed him. If he took his shirt off, she could really see.

Caz repeated, "The package?"

Ashley tossed him the drugstore bag, face on fire, and darted for the door. "It's from the studio," she lied.

Moving fast, Caz caught her arm in a tight grip. He held Ashley in place and upended the bag. The contents fell free.

Thump.

The square, plastic-wrapped box landed face up, centered on the coffee table. The label screamed, *Deluxe Condoms*.

CHAPTER 4

Ashley swallowed and rubbed her free hand across her warm face. Caz, wearing a struck expression, lifted the box of condoms. The plastic wrapping crinkled against his fingers and he gazed from the box to her.

Clearly, she'd surprised him, and if he said anything about the size or type, she'd die. Ashley pulled against his grip, but he held her in place.

Staring at the gift in consideration, he said, "You fancy me?"

She tried to wriggle out of his hold. "What?"

"Are these an invitation?"

Ashley didn't think it was possible to blush any harder, but the heat in her face almost burned. Obviously, Caz didn't buy her story about the studio being behind the purchase. Her voice rushed out. "No. I heard someone say something about sabotaging them. Yours. And I didn't think that was fair, so those are sealed. Use those when you…um…when you, you know."

"Because I'm an actor, I'm off sleeping with everyone?"

Ashley shrugged. "Probably. You movie stars aren't exactly known for your restraint."

Caz frowned. "What exactly did you hear?"

She couldn't tell if he didn't believe her or just wanted to know the whole story, but she wasn't gossiping with an actor. Squirming against his hold, she said, "I may have gotten the story wrong, so I'm not repeating it."

"I want to know what you heard," his clipped British voice commanded.

Ashley stilled. "Contrary to what you think, you can't always get what you want."

"You're quoting song lyrics?"

"British ones," she offered.

A smile edged the corner of his mouth and his fingers loosened. "Tell me." His voice took on a charming, persuasive tone.

Ashley wavered. The new tone in his voice had the power to make her capitulate far more than his commands. Feeling herself weaken, she turned and escaped.

***

Ashley felt Caz's eyes on her, but she avoided him. She didn't want round two of yesterday's embarrassing scene, so she wasn't going near him today. Staying busy kept her away for the first hour.

As soon as Caz realized she was avoiding him, he took matters into his own hands. "PA."

Despite having such short legs, Olive could move quickly. She beat all the other assistants to him. Winning the race didn't score her the prize, though, because Caz waved her off with one word. "Ashley."

Ashley couldn't avoid a direct request; it was her job, so she joined them. "Yeah?"

"I need some assistance."

"With?"

He raised his eyes as if thinking. "Olive, what do you usually assist with?"

Olive gave a little hop. "Anything you need, Mr. Thaymore. I can arrange for food, a change of clothes, cushions for your chair, foot massages."

"PA," the AD called.

Olive looked torn, her eyes darting from the assistant director to Caz, then back, as if trying to judge who was more important. Ashley took a step toward the director and Olive made a hissing sound and pushed past, leaving her with Caz.

Caz chuckled and rose from his chair. He actually had a chair with *Thaymore* embroidered on the back above a shiny gold star. Petra had one too. The rest of the crew took their breaks leaning against the wall or sitting on a crate of equipment, feeling lucky if they were able to grab a crate before they were all occupied.

Caz stretched his arms over his head and leaned side to side. The hem of his shirt rose, showing an inch of his skin. "I probably could use a massage later."

Ashley rolled her eyes. "I have to roll some cable. Your distressed muscles will have to wait."

This pattern continued for the rest of the morning. If another assistant responded to his calls, Caz sent them away, and because Caz was the star, everyone indulged him. If he wasn't directly calling her over, he was staring. Ashley couldn't interpret his looks. Either he wanted to find out more of what she'd overheard, or hook up with her, or maybe both.

During one of his breaks, Caz said, "What's your phone number?"

Ashley sighed. "You don't need my number. I'm always here."

Caz flipped his phone open and examined the screen. "What if I need something after we wrap for the day?"

Ashley bit her lip on what she wanted to answer. Could he do nothing for himself? *Man, these actors were spoiled.* "Guess you'll just have to, oh, oops, sorry, I need to go help Tom with that—" Surely, someone named Tom worked on set. With those words, she left. Olive glared at her as she trotted off, as if trying to determine her destination.

Ashley hadn't gotten very far when she heard the director call, "Powder." A quick glance showed Caz standing in the middle of the set ready for his close-up while stagehands adjusted equipment in the background.

"PA," Caz said.

Ashley walked over to Powder. "I never knew guy actors wore so much makeup."

Powder shrugged and handed over a pre-dusted puff. "No more than my last boyfriend."

Ashley took the powder puff over to the stage area. Holding Caz's hair back, she carefully adjusted his shine. "You need to carry a hair clip in your pocket." His hair felt pretty silky for a guy's and thicker than hers. Idly rubbing a strand between her fingers, she looked over his skin. She couldn't really see the shine problem, but guessed that with high-definition images, it was better to be safe than shiny. On tiptoe, she dabbed at his forehead with the cotton ball. "There you go, shine all gone," Ashley said somewhat condescendingly. Why couldn't he lift the puff to take care of the problem himself?

"Tell me what you heard," Caz said, as she shoved the puff into her pocket.

Okay. He just wanted to hear the reason she'd made the condom purchase. Instead of telling him again, she removed a Chapstick from her other pocket and swiped the balm over his lips. "You have a pretty-shaped mouth. Good thing you're a big guy."

Caz's blue-green eyes brightened, and he leaned toward her. "So the box was just a present then?"

Ashley shook her head.

"Did everyone get one?" Caz looked around. "Shall I ask?"

Ashley stepped back. "Don't make me regret helping you."

"I saw you with a notebook. You're always writing in it. What are you writing?"

"Nothing." The notebook contained her drawings of buildings, and she kept them private; not even Dad had seen her work.

"Are you a writer? Let me guess. You have a script you think is right for me, and are dying to have me read it? Hand the pages over then." Caz held out a raised palm.

"Absolutely, the hero's this total ass who—" Ashley was cut off by the arrival of Petra and her cloud of sultry perfume.

Petra said, "I've got this new belly ring, and I'm not supposed to take the loop out yet, but the AD says gems don't work for the part of the vixen. What do you say?" Petra lifted her shirt up mid-speech, showing the silver ring piercing her belly button. Two star-shaped gemstones hung from a silver hoop. "I think I make the jewelry work."

Powder kneeled for a closer look. "Is your skin infected? The last guy I went out with had a wicked infection in one of his piercings." Powder shook her head. "And I don't think we should cover bacteria with makeup."

Petra made a cut-off squealing noise, and Ashley bit her lip.

Caz stepped back. "You should get that checked out."

"I'll take you to the infirmary," Olive said. "I'm sure if they have to cut the ring out, they can replace the loop with gold. Jewelry looks so great on you. The star makes your stomach look so flat. I want to get a belly ring too."

***

Ashley tried to play it cool, but it was hard to keep the grin off her face. They'd scheduled her to work with the set designer today, a real architect.

Powder pointed him out, a tall thirty-something guy. "Why are you so eager? That job's all dust and cutting."

"I want to be an architect."

Powder wrinkled her nose. "Really? I dated a construction worker once. I'm not sure you want to hang out with those guys."

"Yes. See you later." Ashley went over to the architect with her hand extended. "I'm Ashley, your assistant while you're on set."

"It's usually the actors who are greeted with that kind of smile."

"I don't want to act."

"Another rarity," the architect said then got down to business. Moving across the set, he went over what he wanted to accomplish. After noting her genuine interest and learning she was from Texas, he spoke about dimensions and tensile strength. "Regional earthquakes mean you need strength, or structures will crumple as easily as your bleachers did." He pointed to the beams overhead. "Could be dangerous."

Ashley took copious notes and followed him on his inspection. The set around them buzzed with routine activity, but she didn't let the noise distract her.

"PA?" Caz called from the stage.

Ashley heard him, but ignored the call.

"PA," Caz repeated.

Heaving a sigh, Ashley waved Caz off.

The architect smiled down at her. "Go ahead and take care of our star. I'll be stage left when you're done."

Ashley smiled gratefully then trotted over to Caz. "What?" she asked impatiently, watching the architect.

"Who's that?"

"What do you need? I'm busy."

Caz touched her arm until she met his bright gaze. "You're my assistant."

"Uh, no, I'm not."

He waved a hand in the air. "How long is he going to be here?"

Ashley raised her eyebrows. "Look, do you need something or not?"

"Yes." Caz paused and looked upward as if thinking. "I need to run lines, and my microphone is off, and no one put snacks in my trailer, and—"

Ashley crossed her arms over her chest. "You don't let anyone in your trailer." The architect moved some partitions and tapped on the walls, making Ashley wonder what he was checking.

"And I want—"

Turning back to the needy, Ashley said, "How about this. You leave me alone all morning to work with him, and I'll make sure you have way better snacks in your trailer than the crap provided by the caterer."

Caz flicked a gaze at the architect. "He'll be gone this afternoon?"

She nodded.

"Good snacks?"

"Yes."

"And you'll run lines with me?"

"Can't you run them with your buddy?" His kilt-wearing friend, Garrett, had a supporting role that kept him on the set about once a week, and he was here today.

"He's rubbish at reading the girl parts."

Ashley rolled her eyes.

Caz said, "And you have a nice voice, rich and sweet, but with a kick."

She heaved a mental sigh. "Okay."

***

Powder knelt at a cabinet and shoved large containers aside, digging for something. When Ashley reached her, Powder handed up a large white jug. Ashley placed it on the counter.

Petra flounced into the makeup station and elbowed the jug aside to make room for her laptop. "You have got to see this." The white jug teetered on the edge. "I knew this would happen. I'm always saying, you can't always tell who your friends are. Like when I was vacationing in Madrid, and—"

"What?" Powder asked.

Petra's painted lips grimaced and she poised her finger over the play button. "Check this out."

A polished reporter came on the screen. "I'm Karla Quintos from *Tween In*, online and on the air." She tucked her glossy black hair behind her ears and held a microphone closer to her dark lips. "I'm here to share my interview with screen actor Garrett Campbell. If we're lucky, hopefully, he'll tell us a little bit about what it's like to work with his best friend, the notoriously private Caspian Thaymore."

The scene changed, showing the reporter sitting on a barstool chatting with Garrett. "What's Caspian like?"

"Great fun." Garrett's Scottish accent came through the speakers.

"Are you sure he's not attached?"

Ashley felt someone behind her and looked back. Caz.

His gaze was on the screen.

Garrett said, "Oh no, and he could use some cheering up. A way to drown his tears."

"I may have just the friend to provide the tissue." The reporter touched him on the arm and leaned in. "Are you guys here with your parents?"

Garrett seemed smitten. "We're on our own. I doubt his parents would be here together anyway. They're splitting up, you know."

Ashley glanced at Caz.

The muscle ticked in his jaw and his fists clenched.

***

They broke early that afternoon, and Ashley was eager to get home and try out the new Chinese recipe Marissa had sent. She could never get

Chinese recipes to taste like takeout, but was determined to keep trying. She'd get the stuff for the new dish and pick up ingredients to make Caz's snacks. After winding a last heavy cable, she hung it on the wall and rolled her shoulders back. Time to go home.

Caz stood not too far away, arguing with his tall agent, and the concerned-looking AD hovered nearby. *No peace for the wicked.*

Even though she kept her gaze on the exit and walked with fast steps, Caz snagged her arm when she passed, pulling her into the conversation.

His agent said, "They promised an artistic photo shoot, and you agreed to pose." She patted her pocket as if looking for a cigarette.

Caz shook his head. "I agreed to do press after filming, not during. I should be concentrating on my next scene, practicing my lines."

His agent shrugged and tapped her foot. "You signed the contract. You're committed." She handed Ashley her coffee cup. Ashley stared down at the smelly, empty container.

The AD bounced on the balls of his feet, anxious to please. "We've wrapped for today. You do what you need to do, and we'll send someone to run lines with you."

When photo opportunities emerged, Petra had bionic hearing. She waved at them from her spot on the stage and strolled over. Her ruby-laden belt rolled lower against her hips with each step. "I can be there. I'm already made up, and I have a great relationship with most photographers in town. Only last week, I shot with Rae Frost, you know Rae, right, Rae is famous, after all, well I—"

Ashley wiggled the coffee cup at Caz and smirked.

"PA." Caz quirked an eyebrow. "Go with me."

Ashley shook her head in refusal. She had a ton of things to do other than babysit him.

Petra pouted and curled against Caz's side. She batted her eyelashes until she caught sight of her reflection in a pole, then she went over to the makeup mirror to smooth her hair.

Caz didn't seem to mind that she left. Talkative must not be his type. Ashley wondered if he had a type. Maybe if he had a girlfriend around to cater to some of his whims, she'd have more time to help other crew. She was quickly getting a reputation as "Caz's PA," and the title wasn't winning her any friends. "Couldn't Olive—"

"Olive, over here," the AD said.

Olive pounded her small frame over to them, swinging a hammer in her hand. "How can I help?"

Caz shook his head. "Ashley's got this."

The AD let out a forceful breath. He shoved a script at Ashley. "Pull the car around."

The man obviously saved his coddling tone for the actors.

The agent looked between Olive and Ashley. "I really need that coffee." Her voice was apologetic but insistent.

The AD snagged the cup from Ashley and handed it to Olive. "Get her a fresh one. Then go help out on set B. The mobile toilet's acting up again."

Olive put her head down and beelined for the coffee cart.

Ashley swatted Caz with the rolled script on her way to get the car.

CHAPTER 5

Ashley steered Dad's Audi R8 up to the front of the warehouse and rolled down her window. No way Caz, his agent, plus whomever else was tagging along would fit in her two-seater. They'd have to use a larger car with a studio driver. The studio provided drivers for all the stars, which was wise because actors were notorious for their drunk-driving incidents. Not that she'd seen Caz drunk, but the studio was smart to play it safe. Artistic didn't go hand in hand with reliable.

The agent stood outside with Caz, cradling her new coffee cup and cell phone in the same hand. She eyed the lack of a backseat with a frown and more toe-tapping.

Doing her best to conceal a grin, Ashley spoke through the open window. "Meet y'all there."

"No," Caz said, and went around to the passenger side.

The agent sighed and handed Ashley a card with the photographer's address. "I need him there right away."

"Okay," Ashley said to the agent's narrow back as she walked off. She handed the card to Caz. "Read this into the GPS."

Caz tapped on the upper right hand of the screen, and a feminine voice came on asking for their destination. Caz said, "1342 Water View Road."

Ashley put the car in gear and exited from the front gate onto the streets of Burbank. She glanced at her passenger. "Don't you have a car?"

"I plan to buy one, since I'm staying in the States. I just haven't chosen one yet. This car's nice."

The navigation system asked for a repeat, and Caz said, "1342 Water View Road."

"Thanks. It's my dad's. You should get a big one with a good safety rating since you're not used to driving on the right."

"No."

Ashley pulled over and clicked on the hazard lights, waiting for the GPS to tell her where to go next.

After several beeps, the GPS asked for the address again. Caz leaned close to the navigation screen and spoke the address loudly into the voice activation speaker.

"Please repeat your destination," the female GPS voice said.

Ashley laughed.

Caz narrowed his eyes and tapped on the screen with a forceful index finger. Ashley pushed his hand away and repeated the words in American English.

"Proceed to the intersection. Stay in the right lane."

Caz pursed his lips, glared at the GPS, then turned on the radio. His expression made her grin.

The ride didn't take long, and they reached the photography studio without trouble. Ashley grabbed the script and followed him into the sleek, white, modern interior. The only pop of color came from the smelly eucalyptus plant at the end of the white couch.

His agent bent and smashed a cigarette butt into its mossy base. She was there alone, no Petra or Olive in sight. She'd either driven crazy fast or didn't have to find parking.

The agent shoved her phone in her pocket as Caz drew near, and when they stood within two feet of her, Ashley could tell by the smell that she'd had more than one cigarette with her coffee on the drive over. His agent said, "The shoot's going to be really tasteful."

"Black and white?" Caz asked.

The agent nodded and looked at the receptionist with raised eyebrows and a glance at her watch.

Ashley rolled her eyes and wondered why artists thought color was tacky. She liked color photos. Besides, his eyes were a pretty shade, wasted on black and white.

The receptionist rose from behind a long white half-moon desk and joined them. She stood at least six feet tall, a few inches shorter than Caz. "Mr. Thaymore, we're expecting you. Please proceed to studio two." The receptionist gestured toward the hallway with a slender arm, but her gaze never left Caz.

Studio two had been divided into three areas: technical equipment, makeup, and shooting. Jungle music boomed from speakers mounted in the corners, and a photographer yelled directions over the noise. "Set that up. We need sheets."

Within the makeup area, a tattoo-covered masseuse leaned against a privacy screen that obscured a massage table. She shook a bottle of baby oil at Caz and said, "Over here, cutie. We'll get you prepped for the photo."

Ashley's eyes widened; she couldn't wait to text Marissa about this. "It looks like they're going in a *less* artistic direction," she said.

The agent's mouth twisted at her words and Caz stiffened. The agent shrugged an apology. "It's their right, per the agreement you signed."

Caz looked ready to blow.

The photographer, who was adjusting lenses on set, yelled, "Cover his torso with oil."

Caz didn't move. In fact, he looked like he was one minute from walking out.

The agent patted her jacket for another cigarette. "Come on, Caz, this is important to the film. Besides, you have photo approval. Just do it." The agent stared at Caz for a moment. Her gaze flickered between him and the door then landed on Ashley. She smirked. "His assistant will massage him. Give her the baby oil."

The tattooed masseuse looked disappointed, but she gestured toward the table with an open palm, clearly used to the vagaries of stars. "Coat him waist up." She dropped the bottle of baby oil on the table and followed after Caz's agent. "You know, I'm not just a masseuse, I act too."

Moving over to the table, Ashley lifted the transparent bottle and shook it. The clear gel slid within the container. Caz, who still looked ready to run, nonetheless pulled off his shirt, climbed up to the table, and lay face down.

Ashley took a good look. He was so lean; she hadn't thought he'd be this muscular without his shirt. The director should work in some shirtless scenes to help sell tickets.

His fingers gripped the side of the table and every muscle in his back and arms looked tense.

Ashley opened the lid of the baby oil. *Click.* She sniffed the contents. "You're going to smell like a new diaper." She squirted a blob of oil onto the middle of his back and gave his skin a few tentative slaps, resisting the urge to tap out the jungle beat playing overhead. "My best friend back home's working fast food. So she hasn't been giving me too much sympathy about my summer job." He wasn't tan at all, but his complexion was nice. She smacked a little harder across his shoulders. They felt as hard as a rock. "Marissa's always complaining about the grease from the fry vat."

Sliding an oily hand down his spine, Ashley said, "This is like basting a giant turkey. She's totally going to have some sympathy for me now." Under her hand, he stiffened even more. Ashley spread some of the oil down to his waist. "I'm thirsty. Don't go anywhere, and I'll try to find some water."

Caz said nothing.

Ashley smeared her hand against the side of his arm to lose some of the oil then scooted around the table and out of the screened section. Spotting the agent right away, Ashley asked about drinks.

Motioning toward the set's assistant, the agent said, "We need water and a coffee."

The assistant nodded and took off. It was fun to see someone else scurry for a change.

The agent blew out a breath and tucked her hair behind her ear. "I'm so glad I got Caz to sign this contract while he was distracted, or he'd have never agreed to this shoot." She shot Ashley a conspiratorial look. "Sometimes they need a little push in the right direction. You don't tell them all the details."

That was so not right. The agent was supposed to have his back, not trick him.

The assistant rushed back with some water, saving her the need to reply. Ashley held out her hand, but the assistant hurried past her and around the screen. "It's for Mr. Thaymore." The assistant hovered near Caz and set the bottles on the table. "Let me know if you need anything else, Mr. Thaymore. Anything."

Caz nodded.

Ashley snatched up a bottle. After swallowing some of the cool water, she moved both bottles on the floor. This time she rubbed in the oil with a smooth, pressing motion. His muscles loosened after a few strokes. It was kind of neat. Caz had nice skin, warm, smooth. She flexed her fingers then pushed at his arm. "Over."

Caz flipped and kept his eyes shut.

She paused with the bottle of oil above his chest. He had really defined muscles. The only chest she'd ever touched before had been her last boyfriend. He wasn't six-pack material, and there hadn't been this much touching. Ashley put some of the oil on her palms and rubbed them together to warm the liquid. She laid her fingers against his abdomen.

His eyes flew open. Her fingers stilled. They tingled where they met his skin, and Ashley met his gaze, feeling her face heat. Her mouth opened then shut again. All of a sudden, this felt intimate. She no longer heard the music or the technicians. It was only her cocooned in this small area with Caz, caught in his gaze.

The agent came around the privacy screen. "How's the prep going?"

Withdrawing her hands quickly, Ashley swung them behind her back.

Caz shrugged at the agent and didn't say anything. He sat up and spread the rest of the oil over his torso and arms.

"They're ready for you." The agent rolled her eyes at his silence and went back to the set.

Ashley put a hand against his jean-clad knee and handed him a water. "My friend Marissa works at the Fry Hut, and sometimes she has to wear the French fry costume. She does this minimum wage job to afford things like movies and magazines. So the least you can do is go out there in your baby oil costume and give her a sexy look." She tugged at the seam that ran along the side of his jeans. "It's not like you have to remove your jeans. I'd have your back if they tried to make you strip."

Caz didn't smile, but his mouth twitched a little, and he hopped down from the table. A hairstylist and makeup artist took a few minutes to touch him up, and he was ready to go.

Ashley stayed in the background and watched her first live photo shoot. At first, Caz just stood and stared toward the camera, a shiny image of gorgeous.

Clicking away, the photographer shouted out, "Great, now pout for us. Excellent. Now show us hot." His voice escalated. "Hotter, hotter, make my lens steam. Yes, that's the expression. Now on the bed, drop against the pillows."

Ashley figured the photographer was lucky that Caz's angry looks made him appear sexy; otherwise, it would have been a waste of good film. She kind of got it now, how actors got reputations for being difficult. Caz was blindsided and then told to smile. Life didn't work that way and Caz handled the situation better than she would have.

"Okay, now turn around and shoot us a smoldering look over your shoulder. You're a cave beast. A great man creature. Show us."

Ashley drew in a breath and bit her lip, having to turn away. She couldn't watch with a straight face and doubted the photographer would appreciate her urge to slash her hands through the air with her fingers curled into claws. She felt her hand lift and couldn't resist. She turned to Caz and made a small slash.

A smile eased across his lips.

"Great," the photographer said. "I think we got it."

Caz shook the photographer's hand, grabbed his shirt, and headed straight for the front exit.

Ashley jogged to catch up. "Slow up, man beast."

Caz reached back and grabbed her arm so she'd move faster. Ashley growled. She could see through the glass that the evening had gotten dark outside, and she wondered how he'd take a nocturnal animal joke.

When they went through the door, she was surprised at how quickly the temperature had dropped since they'd arrived. California had such crazy, nice weather. At home, thermostats still read triple digits at ten p.m. Caz shrugged on his shirt one-handed while they walked and only let go of her to get his arm through the sleeve.

Without warning, a bright light flashed, and she stumbled, momentarily blinded. Paparazzi cameras flashed from the sidewalk up ahead. Caz reached back and dragged her forward.

CHAPTER 6

The paparazzi stood between them and the parking lot. She should have had Caz wait inside while she drove the car around. She'd know next time.

"Let's go," Caz said. Heads down, they ran all-out to the car.

Holding up the keyless entry, Ashley chirped open the locks as soon as they were in range. After speeding out of the lot, she said, "Maybe it's good you have a driver. Photographers are crazy." She slowed to make the turn and said, "What am I thinking? You're an actor. Do you want me to circle back around so they can get more shots?"

"No."

Caz checked his phone and frowned.

"What?"

He didn't answer.

Shut into the tiny car with him, she could really smell the baby oil. She decided to give him a break. "I wish my friend Marissa didn't have to work all summer and could come up. You bringing anyone over?"

Silence. Then he said in a gravelly voice, "Didn't you see the news?"

Oops, of course she had. His friend Garrett spilled the news about his parents' split on air. "Do you want to talk about what happened?"

He shook his head.

Ashley said, "At least Garrett's here, when you decide to forgive him, that is."

Caz frowned and shifted in his seat. "Never happen."

Ashley sucked in a breath. "A lifelong friendship and you're giving up after one mistake?"

"Fool me once."

Okay, one shot and you're out; that sounded like Hollywood. She didn't think she could keep a friend who wouldn't allow her to make a mistake. Everyone made mistakes. Actors made lots of them. Ashley braked for the red light.

They rode in silence for a few blocks and then Ashley tried for a new topic. "Marissa sent me a new recipe, but I can't get it to taste as good as takeout. I'll have to call her when I get home and see what ingredient is missing." She chatted about Marissa's creative recipes for the rest of the trip.

Caz looked kind of expectant right up to the point where she parked near his trailer. Putting one hand on the door handle, he raised his eyebrows at her. "Did you want to get dinner?"

Please, twelve hours on set were enough. She really hadn't been hitting on him with the condoms. He needed to let that go. "Too busy, but you have a good night."

"Good night."

***

The assistant director caught her as Ashley walked into the warehouse the next morning. "They need you in the filing room, warehouse twelve."

Olive stood in the background, nodding. She held a tray of coffee cups with one empty slot. A matching cup rested in the AD's hand.

Olive said, "I've got this set covered. You go ahead and file."

Ashley turned back to the door. "No problem."

Olive's hurried stomps caught up to her. "Coffee?" she asked loudly. Ashley shook her head. Olive knew she didn't like coffee. Olive leaned close and whispered, "Sleeping with someone may have gotten you the job, but I guess whoring won't save you from filing."

"What? That wasn't part of your interview too?"

Olive's hazel eyes glowered. "I'll go do my job now. You have no idea how much I have to do around here."

"Who do you think I slept with?"

"We all know." Olive scooted back and pounded her way to the coffee cart.

Ashley detoured by the makeup station. While walking, she shot off a text to Marissa. "Hollywood gossip says I slept with someone to get this job."

Marissa texted, "It's an unpaid internship. You must not be very good at it."

Ashley smiled and felt some of her tension ease. "What do I do?"

The reply returned immediately. "Fry vat overflowed. Irina suggested I still serve the floor fries. Tell gossiper what I told her."

Ashley texted, "What did you stick in the oil?"

"Whole potatoes, cored and stuffed with special seasoning. Customers rated 'em an eight."

***

Ashley left the drama behind her in search of warehouse twelve. It stood near the stucco main office buildings. Ashley jogged past and headed to Dad's office. She took the elevator to the top floor. Tap, tap, tap. "Dad in?" she asked his secretary.

"Sorry, dear, he's got meetings all day."

Ashley swallowed and backtracked to warehouse twelve. A gray-haired woman sat at a long counter inside with row upon row of floor-to-ceiling racks behind her. Fluorescent bulbs hummed overhead, and the smell of dusty paper overwhelmed the space.

"I'm Ashley Herrington, here to assist for the day."

The woman slowly raised her eyes from the papers in front of her and gestured behind her. Ashley moved around the counter. Boxes of papers were stacked under the counter and on the floor all around her chair. The lady lifted a piece of paper, stared at the words, then wrote a number in the top right corner. Then she put the coded piece of paper in an outbox to her left. She nudged the outbox toward Ashley. "File these. The shelves and folders are numbered."

Ashley lifted the papers and headed into the world of filing. Minutes in the world of filing crawled by like the Dallas Cowboys in the fourth quarter—slow. She really needed to thank Dad for getting her the job on the set instead of in an office because this was painful. Ashley checked the clock on the wall. It had to be almost noon. The clock read nine forty-five. She swallowed and trekked back to the front. "Are there any vending machines near here?"

The gray head shook. "They didn't want to risk anything getting wet. Or people taking too many breaks."

"So no restroom either?"

"You have to go two buildings over for that."

Ashley went back to row 844 to continue filing and played tunes on her mobile phone until the battery ran down. She filed everything she could, and the only things left in her pile were ones labeled with a number and the letter *B*. Ashley jogged back to the front. "I can't find row 72B."

The gray-haired lady let her hand drape off the counter and she pointed downwards. "Below this floor. Sub-basement filing."

Noon.

Thank you, God. Ashley climbed up from the basement storage and dropped off the empty outbox with the filing lady. The filing lady didn't say thanks. Ashley waved anyway and ran for the exit. She threw her arms out in the California air, blinked against the sunlight, and sucked in a breath free of the smell of paper.

Odd how just being in a filing room could make you so thirsty. Maybe it was California's dry air; or maybe it was the knowledge that the building didn't have a drink machine. She couldn't have a drink, so she wanted a drink—the lure of the forbidden.

In addition to boredom and thirst, the repetitive task of filing in the cold basement had made her stiff. Here she was, living in the land of yoga, and she could barely move. Stretching on tiptoe to work out her muscles, she spotted a new coffee kiosk and went to see if they had hot chocolate.

They did, but they also had hot tea. In Texas, she only liked iced tea, but California got chilly, so hot tea worked. Craft services offered tea on set, but theirs tasted like the bottom of the coffee pot they brewed it in, so she'd only drank it once.

She stirred in milk and sugar and popped on the white lid. The steam of the tea seeped through the hole. Sipping the drink, she made the short walk back, enjoying the warmth of the cup against her cold fingers. Inside, the stage area was quiet, which meant shooting. She eased closer.

"Cut," the director said, right as Ashley got close enough to watch.

Ashley hoped they'd resume soon. When Caz transformed into character, his eyes changed, his posture changed. He became the part, intense, amazing. She never told him because he had enough praise. Olive usually began the compliments, but others chimed in. He didn't need her gushing too.

"Caz, sorry to hear about your parents," the director said. "If you're going to need time off during the shoot, we need to schedule the break now."

Caz waved a dismissive hand. "It's fine, Russ."

"I know how hard divorce can be," the director said. "My ex-wife still calls every week, needing something. Plus, Garrett will be on set again soon for more shooting."

Caz's face took on a detached expression. "Not a problem."

The director looked like he would say more, but Caz left him and joined Ashley. He took her cup and sipped. He blinked and his shoulders relaxed. "Tea."

Fetching him a drink and having him take hers were two different things. Staking her claim, Ashley took the tea back from him and took a drink. She held his gaze while she did it.

Caz frowned, and spoke with a heavier British accent than he normally used. “Where’d you get it then?”

Ashley raised an eyebrow. “That’s for me to know and you to find out.” She stroked a finger down the side of the cup. “Yum.”

“That’s rubbish. I know that’s not from this set.”

***

After that episode, it became routine for Caz to drink out of her drinks, sort of a game on his part. He grinned every time she took the cup back and drank after him. Just this morning, he’d snagged her cup on her way to the makeup area.

Powder handed her a stack of application brushes and numbered sticky labels. “He’s flirting,” she said. She wore an orange sherbet dress with matching tights and she spoke with authority. “I had an ex who liked to steal my stuff. He only stole to stay near me.”

“He’s not.”

Powder nodded, and placed the numbered items on a tray. Every now and then, she’d glance at some notes or a Polaroid photo to make sure she knew which scenes they were shooting, whose makeup she’d be doing, and what that makeup looked like when they’d left off the last scene.

There were separate makeup areas set up for minor actors and extras, but Powder did all the key players except Petra. Petra had her own makeup artist, and only came by the makeup chairs for a touchup or some gossip.

Ashley loaded the next tray, fiddling with one of the face creams. “Is it creepy touching strangers?”

“Nah, I’ve dated worse than these guys.”

Ashley fluffed a soft brush against her palm and sat on one of the folding chairs. “Who’s the worst?”

“It’s all good as long as the actor’s not one of those free spirits who refuse to shower and won’t use deodorant. I’ve worked on a few of those.”

“Great,” Ashley said. “I hope I get to work on someone who’s had a shower.”

Caz came around the partition and took the seat beside her. He wore a frown and his head tilted downwards. Actors had expressive faces, and his read annoyed. Ashley wondered if he needed breakfast. Maybe she should take care of that before his makeup.

Two other actors came over. Powder pointed them into chairs and tossed a jar of face cream toward Ashley.

Ashley caught the heavy glass container and Powder gestured toward Caz. "Put that on his face and neck. I've got these two."

Opening the lid, Ashley took a sniff. Not bad, a faint rose fragrance. Sticking her finger into the pink cream, she scooped some onto the back of her hand: cool, wet. She set the jar on her armrest and got up. "Hi," she said; then she rubbed the cream between her hands. "Did you get breakfast?"

Caz ignored her question. "I took a shower. Just because I'm British doesn't mean I don't shower."

Ashley tilted her head at him. What a leap. She hadn't been talking about him. "Maybe you do, maybe you don't. Let me see." Leaning forward until her elbows rested on the wooden armrests of his chair, she put her face near his shoulder and neck, and made snuffling sniffs. He smelled like ocean wave soap and shampoo. "You'll do."

Caz shot her a little glare that made her laugh, and Powder said, "Stop sniffing him and get to work." She'd already moved on to the next stage of makeup application.

Ashley leaned back. Using one hand, she braced against his chair and leaned forward to rub some cream into his face. Because of his height, leaning over his knees and reaching up to his face was awkward. She looked over to see Powder's method.

Powder was tall too. There wasn't a trick; she stood beside the actors' chairs and behind their chairs and pretty much just got in their personal space. Ashley scooped up some more cream and looked at Caz, assessing the best angle.

Caz put his hands on her waist and pulled her forward. When her jean-clad legs hit his, he tugged one of her knees up until it rested on his chair beside his thighs.

"Thanks." Ashley used one hand and pulled up until she straddled his legs. The fabric director's-style chair made balancing a little difficult, so she mostly sat on his lap. "Security let me in your trailer this morning."

Caz frowned.

"I dropped off snacks."

His eyes flickered. "Thanks."

She rubbed the cream onto his face, then his neck. Tucking her fingers into the neckline of his V-neck, she pressed into the top of his shoulders, kneading. He shifted toward her and put his hands on her waist to help her balance when she kneeled up to reach lower. His skin was warm and his muscles hard.

Caz's hands held Ashley in place, and occasionally, he'd rub his thumbs over her waist. Sensation radiated out whenever his fingers moved, and her eyelids lowered, making concentrating on the makeup application difficult.

Powder said, "Uh, Ashley, that's good enough."

Ashley looked in Powder's direction, her hands still in Caz's shirt. "Hmm?"

Powder smirked. "Face and neck are fine."

Ashley slowly removed her hands from his shirt and contracted her fingers.

Powder rolled a tray over. "Watch while we add a little street makeup, to make him look natural under the lights." Her hand swiped quickly along Caz's face with a brush dipped in concealer. The makeup artist concentrated on her task, but she talked to Ashley the whole time. "Do you have a boyfriend? Or like any boy back in Texas?"

"No," Ashley said. "After my last breakup, I picked out a new guy named Kevin, but I couldn't catch him."

Powder added Chapstick. "I've never dated a Kevin."

Ashley stayed on Caz's lap and watched closely. They'd definitely shoot a close-up of Caz's mouth because the shape was perfectly proportioned, not too thin, definitely one of his best features, and that was saying something. Caz had naturally dark lashes, so Powder left those untouched.

"I'll tell you about the Kissing Pentagon," Powder said. "Once you perfect the technique, try the pentagon on him." Eyeliner came next. Powder applied eyeliner then lightened the line with the end of a cotton swab.

"Perfect it?"

"Pick a guy." Powder waved toward the studio. "Use one of 'em. Those boys back in Texas won't know what hit them."

"I can't randomly kiss some guy."

"Fine, then pick a guy friend." Last, Powder added a dusting from a compact.

Caz looked at Powder with bored expectation. Ashley caught the look and could tell he thought Powder would name him—actors and their egos.

Powder said, "Boomer would kiss you."

CHAPTER 7

Boomer rolled up his sleeves to better display his arms. Once his sleeves were up, he lifted his hands overhead to hold on to the metal boom pole. The muscles in his arms bulged, huge. Ashley tilted her head to get a better look.

Caz squeezed his hands at her waist, drawing her attention back to him.

"Hmm?"

Caz didn't respond, but his eyes focused on hers.

"You're done," Powder said.

At those words, Ashley hopped up and looked back at Boomer, wondering what he did at the gym to get that physique. He had to work out at least twice a day, maybe more.

Caz stood and stepped in front of her, interrupting her thoughts. "I need you to get something from my trailer."

Ashley waited two seconds with eyebrows raised, but he didn't say anything more. "Don't the British know the magic word?"

Caz used his rich compelling voice. "Please."

"Ooh." Powder made a sound of appreciation. "Or, you could try a kiss out on him."

Ashley looked away from Caz toward the source of Powder's awe.

Garrett stood near the entrance, looking like the cover of a highland-themed romance novel in his green kilt. He swaggered forward, heading their way, moving like a male model on the catwalk. Garrett nodded toward a female stagehand, but didn't stop to talk. He walked and kept his flirt on at the same time.

Caz's mouth tightened, and he crossed his arms over his chest.

Garrett stepped into the makeup station and looked at Caz. "Are you going to ever answer your phone again?"

Caz turned his back on Garrett. Garrett reached out and grabbed Caz's shoulder. "Listen."

Caz threw a hard elbow into Garrett's restraining arm, breaking the grip. Garrett's left fist swung at Caz's face.

Powder screamed, "Not the face."

"Stop," Ashley yelled.

Caz lowered his shoulder and moved into the swing. The punch grazed the air, missing Caz, and the momentum knocked Garrett off balance. His big body wheeled backwards, his feet tangling in a hair dryer cord. He took out one of Powder's makeup carts as he crashed to the ground. A puff of peach shimmer plumed into the air and all the labeled products tangled together.

Powder stepped between the fighters, hands on her hips. "I just sorted those!"

Garrett laughed. "Sorry, darling." He raised onto his elbows, facing Caz with a wince. "Will you listen to me now? I thought the reporter fancied *me*, not an interview."

Caz stalked off before Garrett finished. The Scottish actor dusted off his palms and spoke to the empty space where Caz had stood. "I was just chatting her up. I didn't know she was taping me."

***

Having run an errand across the lot, Ashley returned carrying two cups of tea. Caz stood beneath the lights with the other actors, so she propped his cup on his star chair.

Boomer, wearing a tank shirt, worked the microphone over the stage. Petra gave him several looks. He didn't notice though because his gaze was glued to his arms. When the scene cut, Ashley raised her eyebrows. "Need a break?"

Boomer nodded. "Thanks." He removed his earphones and hooked them around her neck.

The boom microphone was an additional one on this set. The microphone hung from the end of a long overhead pole attached to a vertical upright pole. They called the equipment the fishing pole. She knew what to do. Keep the microphone over the lead actors while they shot the scene. Since Boomer had shown her what to do, Ashley occasionally gave him a break, but this wasn't her favorite task.

She set her own cup down and took hold. The pole was lightweight, but her upper body strength and height weren't a fraction of Boomer's. She'd worked with him one full Saturday, and holding her hands in that position for long periods of time had made her arms shake; Boomer had earned the right to be proud of his biceps. Ashley blew her bangs out of her eyes. The position also explained why Boomer buzzed his hair short.

Olive never gave him a break. Confining her assistance to the directors and the leads, Olive honed her importance. To be fair, though, the pole was set high today. Olive wouldn't be able to reach it without a stepping stool.

Today's pole position caused Ashley to raise her arms straight over her head so high that her shirt rose up, leaving a distinct gap between the hem and the top of her low-rise jeans. She hoped Boomer was quick in the bathroom. With luck, he'd return before they started the next scene. Ashley released the pole and stood ready for the director's call.

Caz stepped in front of her and bent to pick up her cup. Ashley watched him, with her hands on her hips, while he sipped. "I brought you one. Yours is in your chair."

Caz shrugged. "Garrett took mine."

Before she met Caz, she thought the British love of tea was a joke, but their obsession appeared to be true. She took the cup from Caz and drank, using her eyes to dare him to say anything.

Beep. Caz checked his phone and muttered before turning off the ringer.

"Who's that?"

He shrugged and took the cup from her for another drink. "Show me your tea source."

"You have a trailer with a kitchenette."

Caz shrugged again.

"Fine, let me know when you have a break. We'll need at least twenty minutes."

Caz's eyes brightened. "We can—"

Sipping from the cup intended for Caz, Garrett joined them. Ashley narrowed her eyes and shook her head at the tea thief.

Garrett grinned around the white plastic lid. "I prefer tea with extra sugar, no milk."

"It wasn't yours," Caz said.

Ashley looked at Caz pointedly as he sipped from her cup—like he had any room to point fingers.

"Maybe the darling boom girl here could bring one for me," Garrett said with a thickened Scottish accent, his twinkling mint-green eyes staring at her.

"There's no tea on…" Ashley started to explain, but Caz cut her off.

"No. She's my PA."

Garrett's eyes widened, and he slowly grinned before moving closer to Ashley. "Well maybe, PA darling, on your off hours, you can show me around LA. I'm here this week. I rarely get out to California. California girls…"

Garrett sung the next verse until Caz shut down the musical performance. Caz said, "She's from Texas. And we're busy."

Ashley rolled her eyes, amazed that Caz thought he could answer for her.

Garrett swirled the cup in his hand while he taunted Caz. "I read you've been extra busy since your girlfriend gave birth to twins."

Ashley's eyes widened, but Caz shook his head. "Tabloid lies. You like those, don't you?"

"Or maybe it's because you've been so busy trying to date both actresses on set, Lorene and Petra. I read about that too."

His Scottish accent really dragged out the *O*'s in the word *too*; the sound made Ashley want to purse her lips and imitate him, but she wasn't a natural mimic. She bet Caz could copy the accent. She looked at Caz's lips in assessment. Caz's pretty mouth said something foul in Garrett's direction. Garrett laughed in delight.

"Positions," the AD said.

Garrett moved into place for the scene. Caz waited until Garrett was away before putting down Ashley's cup. She took hold of the pole and asked him, "Can you do a Scottish accent?"

"Noooo," Caz said in perfect imitation. Then he joined the other actors under the lights.

Ashley smiled and maneuvered the pole so the microphone hovered into position. The hem of her shirt rose again, exposing several inches of her midriff, but she couldn't do anything about the display and perform her job at the same time. Garrett's gaze seemed to settle on her waist every time he peered off in the distance. She could only frown. Caz caught the stares too. His annoyance worked well with the scene.

Midway through, Boomer returned to take over; his eyes were on her waist too. She relinquished the pole with a smile. He earned his keep. That pole hurt. Swinging her arms to stretch them, she walked over to Powder's station. After climbing on the makeup counter, she used her free time to sketch in her notebook.

"Take two hours," the AD called. Some days they got fifteen minutes for lunch, some days they got a couple of hours.

Ashley grinned at Powder. "Cool."

Powder pursed her lips around a secret smile and she trotted toward the exit. She'd started dating a new man and was uncharacteristically quiet about this one, not even divulging his name. Ashley hoped, whoever he was, that he'd at least finished his parole. She put her notebook in her bag and shouldered the strap, planning to follow Powder's lead and get away from the set.

"Want to grab Chinese fried rice with chicken?" Garrett asked. "Or find some kind of chocolate truffle cake with a vanilla frosting?"

Caz stopped just behind Garrett. "We have plans."

Ashley lifted an eyebrow. "We do?"

Caz made a drinking motion with his hand. "Yes, you promised."

Ashley smiled. Caz would be great at charades. "Oh yeah. Thanks anyway, Garrett."

"Well," Garrett said, nodding at Caz, "you and your bird, have a nice—break."

Caz flipped Garrett off and reached for her hand to tug her away.

Ashley raised an eyebrow.

"Bird?"

"Girl."

"You're not calling me that." Ashley pointed toward the mediocre catering cart with her free hand. "Want a sandwich?"

Caz shook his head. "Do you?"

Wrinkling her nose, Ashley shook her head too. The only days she ate cart food were the fifteen-minute lunch days. Even then, she sometimes heated something up from home. Other days, she ate nearby with one of the crew and, once, she caught up with her dad and had lunch with him.

"Hey, Caz," Cutter said. "Buddy, why don't we hit the executive lounge? You can get us in." He wore skinny jeans with a metallic silver shirt. The silver shimmered with each demand.

"He's got plans." Ashley tightened her grip on Caz's hand. Cutter made a twisty face at her, but she didn't care. She didn't normally take up for Caz, but this wasn't the first time she'd heard a crew member ask him a favor. She'd heard requests for screen time, a trip to Vegas, and introductions to female fans. She hoped British people imposed on him too, so it wasn't just an American thing. Maybe users were just a Hollywood thing; that was probably true, classic Hollywood.

Caz smiled at her and pulled her arm close to his side. They hadn't walked much closer to the exit before Olive intercepted them. "Need any help with your fan mail? I have a free hour and could start on yours. I do Petra's."

Caz said, "No. Thank you, though."

Ashley saw another crew member headed their way. She turned away from the main exit and led Caz to a side door. On the seven-minute journey that ended at the coffee and tea kiosk, he didn't release her arm, and she had to lengthen her steps to keep up with him. His breath sucked in when he spotted the cart and its large display of colored tea packets.

Caz poked through the selection with an intensity usually reserved for typing in nuclear detonation codes. In the end, he went with the black Earl Grey.

As the attendant handed over the cup, a set of brakes squealed on one of the large tourist carts. The driver whizzed to a stop at the side of the kiosk. The dozen or so tourists offloaded and swarmed around them, reaching for menus, yelling out questions. They appeared to be half families and half couples.

She could tell the moment they recognized Caz. Their murmurs got louder and their sunglasses swiveled away from thc drink menu. Caz tossed his stir stick in a nearby trash bin and turned to go back to the set, seeming oblivious to the dozen gazes now glued to him.

Ashley put a hand on his arm. “Aren’t you even going to say hi and shake a few hands?”

Caz shook his head. “Most girls are annoyed when I leave them to greet fans.”

Ashley rolled her eyes. “My friends *are* your fans. I’d be annoyed if you couldn’t spare three minutes.”

Caz turned back to the group. “Hi.”

The tour guide froze and then rushed to Caz’s side and spoke with an important voice. “This, ladies and gentlemen, is Caspian Thaymore, star of *Eternal Loss, Eternal Revenge*. Filming now.”

Ashley’s lips quirked. They’d already recognized Caz, so the tour guide’s intro was overkill.

One brave kid, about ten, held up a napkin and a pen. Caz didn’t hesitate. He signed the beaming kid’s autograph then shook a few hands and chatted a bit with each person about the tour, the weather, and tea. He even posed for photos. After he’d met each person, Ashley held her phone to her ear like someone called, went over, and said with her best serious voice, “You’re needed back on set, Mr. Thaymore.”

Caz nodded, waved, and left behind a group of wowed fans.

“That was so cool,” Ashley said.

Caz threaded his free arm though hers and Ashley let him. “What?”

“That they recognize your talent and then you made them so happy.” She squeezed his big hand and walked closer to his side. “Good job.”

“So you think I’m talented?” Caz tilted his chin at a cocky angle.

Ashley grinned but refused to respond; that was enough praise for now. She lightly closed her eyes for a second, enjoying the cool, dry air and the moment.

Caz’s steps slowed as they neared their warehouse, and he said, “We should get something to eat.”

Ashley checked the time on her cell phone. An hour and a half remained for lunch, plenty enough time to go out. She tugged loose and stepped toward the parking lot. "Okay, see you on set."

"Let's get something together."

Ashley shook her head. "The press would mob you. I'll get takeout and bring something back. What would you like?"

Caz shrugged and looked away. His free hand formed a fist and he stuffed it into his pocket. "I'm always stuck in that trailer."

If she didn't know him better, she'd say he wore a pout. Low blood sugar always made people cranky. Ashley said, "Price of fame," but this time with some sympathy. She'd be sick of the trailer too.

Caz stepped closer. "I don't have to get out of the car."

"Fine, come on. Dad's Audi has tinted windows anyway."

With her agreement, his good mood restored itself.

"You could wear a wig disguise or something," Ashley said as they got in.

"People don't bother me as much as you think." Caz's seatbelt clicked on and he leaned against the headrest.

"I know LA. It's a feeding frenzy. My dad's dated actresses before. *Nightmare.* I'd never do it." Ashley turned on the radio.

Caz put his left arm on the console and thumped his hand against the side of the door. "I don't like dating actresses either."

Ashley laughed. "What do you want for lunch?"

"Umm, dockside fish and chips or a west-end pub."

"Homesick?" Taking her right hand from the steering wheel, she touched his arm lightly. He took her hand in his and rubbed his thumb over the top, and Ashley noted the incongruity of rough fingertips below buffed fingernails. "When will you go back?"

"No time. My agent keeps the projects booked back to back."

"They have great seafood in California. You should go over to Santa Monica or drive up the coast if you're missing fish and chips."

"They have great fish and chips?"

"No, but the view's so pretty, they seem awesome. Even the tofu sauce." Ashley hit the blinker and turned into the back parking lot of a nearby restaurant. Huge bougainvilleas edged the border, aiding in customer privacy. She found a spot as close as possible to the back door, and shook her hand free to put the car in park.

"This place is fairly dark and you order at the counter," Ashley said, getting out of the car. "We used to take one of my dad's model girlfriends here when she didn't want to be recognized. I can put you in a dark booth then place our orders."

Caz nodded. He was less demanding off set than on, but then again he had gotten his way. Ashley crossed the pavement and reached the back entrance to the off-white stucco building. "Lunch here's worth a shot, but I won't make any promises that you won't get recognized and trampled."

Caz pushed the door open and held it while she went through. "It's not my trailer or a set sandwich. I'm thrilled."

Inside the restaurant, the aroma of tomatoes, Mexican spices, and a sizzling grill filled the room. Caz kept his head down and averted while following her to a back booth. He slid across the cracked, red vinyl first, and Ashley handed him a menu to hold in front of his face.

"I'll surprise you, unless you know what you want?"

Caz shook his head and spoke with firm words, "Anything other than diet sandwich on wheat."

Ashley grinned. She'd made the wheat mistake once. The sawdust on set looked and probably tasted better than that meal. After ordering a variety, she slid in the booth beside him, providing more cover. "This is California Mexican. Be warned, the food's not TexMex."

"Everything's better in Texas?"

"You know it. What would you really be eating if you were in London?"

Caz told her a little about his favorite restaurants and she talked some more about home. After their buzzer went off, Ashley fetched their lunch and slid the heavy tray in front of him. "Don't get used to being served. This is just so we don't get stampeded."

"Thanks." Caz offloaded the dishes and passed the tray across the table. He took a sip of his drink and carefully sampled the food.

Ashley bit into a tortilla chip covered in salsa, happy to have Mexican food even if the recipes weren't as good as home. "I'm so jealous of your architecture in Europe. After I graduate, I'm going to tour some of your European cities and stare. What do you recommend?"

Caz told her stories, and she told him about her plans to major in architecture.

Beep. The alarm on her phone signaled time to depart. "Wow, okay, we gotta go."

Caz glanced at his watch with a frown and nodded. When they reached the back exit, he leaned forward and pushed the metal bar in, holding the door for her.

They got back without incident and Ashley pulled the car as close as she could get to the warehouse entrance, and put on her hazard lights. "I'll drop you here."

"Go ahead and park. I'm British, we like to walk."

Ashley shook her head. "They'll kill me if you're late. You should go in."

Caz paused a moment, then got out.

Ashley clicked off the hazard lights and put the car in gear. "That was fun though, thanks for joining me."

"It was quite good."

"You'll have to go back when you get your car."

"We could go this weekend," Caz said.

"Can't. Mom's in town for a long weekend. I'm so psyched. We're going to check out some universities."

Caz held onto the doorframe, and his eyes took on a distant expression. "Your mom's staying with you and your dad?"

"They get along great." Ashley softened her voice. "Not all divorces are bad."

Caz tapped the side of his phone. His face blanked and he shut the door. "Tell that to my parents."

***

Ashley went over to Powder when she finally got a break. Mondays were a killer.

Powder said, "How was your weekend with your mom?"

"Normal. Fun. Dad even showed up for dinner two nights in a row."

Powder shook her head and her giant hoop earrings swung, making tiny parrots do a 360-degree spin off the bottom of the hoops. "I don't get divorced people who still like each other. I've had to get more than one restraining order against my exes. That's passion."

Ashley didn't respond to that theory. "How'd your weekend go?"

"I got stood up. His buddies were in town and wanted to pull some all-night road trip to Vegas. But don't worry; I'll make him pay before I forgive him. "

"You should try dating normal sometime."

Ashley gestured to Boomer lugging a chair under each arm. He plopped them down side by side.

"What's that?"

"A reporter'll be here later," Powder said.

Ashley raised her eyebrows.

"She's going to interview Caz, Petra, and Lorene. They're calling the segment *Eternal Loss, Eternal Revenge's Trinity of Stars*."

"Hmm. I haven't met Lorene."

"Me either."

Lorene was the supporting actress booked to play Caz's long-lost love. She hoped she liked Lorene more than she liked Petra. It wouldn't take much.

Powder made a ticked sound when she found a cotton swab in with the lip liner brushes. For a wild person, she was crazy organized.

Powder put her hands on her hips. "I'm missing a frosted cream pencil in aquamarine and a ruby slush lip liner. That's the last time Olive helps me." She stomped toward the back exit. "Olive. Where are you?"

"Give me a hand here?" Boomer called. Ashley joined him. He shoved a coffee table in front of one of the chairs and frowned more. "It's supposed to look cozy for the star's interviews. What's cozy?"

Cutter, walking by, frowned. "Not that."

Ashley ignored Cutter and tugged one of the chairs around so that they faced the other.

Boomer centered the small coffee table between the two chairs.

Cutter returned carrying blankets. He tucked the throw over the back of the chair. "Lorene goes first." He handed Ashley a blue and red blanket. "Then Caspian, and then Petra. Switch out the backdrops for each." Cutter smoothed the fabric into place. "Green will complement Lorene's peaches-and-cream coloring."

Olive pounded over and plopped a tea tray on the coffee table. "When's Lorene getting here?"

Cutter shrugged, and his gaze swiveled around the set. "She should be here. I need to fit her dress." His left eye twitched and he snagged a sugar cube from the bowl.

Olive slapped at his hand. "Those are for Caspian." She adjusted a tiny teapot and arched an eyebrow at Ashley.

"Ash." The AD walked up, waving a roll of colored tape her way.

"I got the blocking done earlier," Ashley said. The actors were blocking today, so she had come in early to stick tape on the floor, marking the actors' spots, one color for Lorene, one color for Caz.

Olive ran to the AD. She snagged the tape from his hand and stomped over to the stage. She scoured the floor, putting slightly larger pieces of tape over the already marked spots.

Today was going to be a sixteen-hour day for sure. Ashley had typed up a text message warning Dad she'd be late, though he usually worked even later than she did. "Hey, Boomer," Ashley said.

"Yeah?" Boomer sat on a crate threading the wire for a hidden microphone through a vase.

"The interviews are going to be over there, in a second." Ashley gestured with her free hand toward the cozy nook he'd set up.

"You need mics?"

"No, but you should move your crate against that wall or hang that cable back there. Get seen on camera, maybe. You're too out of the way over here."

Color flooded his face and his buzzed head ducked. "Maybe."

Ashley's mouth dropped. She thought he'd love to invite a million viewers to the gun show. Who knew?

A new woman walked on set. Movie sets were a crazy rush of people all the time but since they worked such long hours, Ashley knew most of the crew. She recognized the new woman from her online interview with Garrett; and if she hadn't, she'd have guessed she was a reporter by her shellacked hair, toothy grin, and navy suit.

Ashley frowned. Caz was expecting a professional newscast. *Tween In* was a show for teens and younger, one step up from a tabloid wanting to discuss his alien baby. What was his agent thinking? He was going to hate this interview. She peeked at the clock on her cell phone. Lorene was due, but no Lorene. She'd better get Caz ready to go early.

Caz stood by the tea tray. His hand reached for a teacup, an unsuspecting look on his face.

Stilling his hand, Ashley said, "Let me." She gestured for him to take a seat and poured him a cup with milk and sugar. Before handing the porcelain to him, she whispered, "You know about the interview, right?"

"Yes, an entertainment segment for a news program." Caz took a sip and smiled at the cup. "I'm going to talk about my character's descent from happiness to emptiness."

Ashley nodded. "Powder said the director's going to contrast the memories of your lost love's sweetness against the vixen's manipulations."

Caz slumped and rested the cup on the arm of the chair. "It's a change to have a good script to discuss. One that's complete before we start shooting."

She smiled. Dad had told her horror stories of unfinished scripts and impossible deadlines.

The reporter, her cameraman, and the AD joined them. Caz rose, and Ashley stepped out of the way while they exchanged greetings.

"I'm Karla Quintos from *Tween In,* online and on the air," the reporter said without smudging her shiny pink lipstick.

Caz's smile faltered for a second then returned.

The two sat down and Caz offered the reporter tea. She declined and got straight down to it. Facing her camera, she said, "We're here on the set of *Eternal Loss, Eternal Revenge* with the hottest star on the planet, Caspian Thaymore. Caspian. Your fans are dying to know—boxers or briefs?"

CHAPTER 8

Oh. That was not going to go over well. Ashley sucked in a breath and bit her lip.

Caz stared at the reporter a long moment then ignored her question. "I'm really enjoying my stay in California. The weather is lovely." Caz sat a little straighter.

Good save, a British fallback to the weather.

"Brunettes or redheads?" the reporter asked, undeterred. She was clearly hinting for him to say which costar he liked best: the brunette Petra or the redheaded Lorene. Tabloid rumors were running rampant about his dating each of them.

Putting his teacup down, Caz said, "Blondes."

"That's so cute, but a reputable source says you've been smooching on set with the redheaded Lorene. So spill the juicy details."

Caz glanced at his watch, the door, and the AD. "Lorene Dailer hasn't arrived on set, so that makes that rumor highly improbable."

"What's your favorite color?"

Caz maintained his smile. "The director is doing amazing things with this script and the juxtaposition of the characters."

The reporter stiffened and spoke slowly, "This is very important. Do you tweet?"

"No."

"You don't mind if I touch that famous jaw, do you?" The reporter lifted a hand toward Caz's face. Caz stiffened and lost his smile, but stayed still while the reporter ran her manicured fingers over his square chin and along his jaws.

Ashley winced.

Eyeing Caz uneasily, the AD pointed at his watch and spun his index finger, a signal to the reporter to wrap up the interview.

"One last question, Caspian. We know who your character loves. But who would Caspian himself most like to marry—sweet and true or the sultry vixen?" The reporter drew out the last two words and wiggled her eyebrows.

Caz pursed his lips. He shot a quick glance over at Ashley then back to the reporter. "My PA. She's a great cook."

Ashley rolled her eyes in the background. Way to set the women's movement back fifty years, Caz.

"There you have it, tweens. Caspian wants a blonde who can cook. I know I'll be going out to buy peroxide and sign up for cooking lessons. See you in class. Signing off from the set of *Eternal Loss, Eternal Revenge*, I'm Karla Quintos and you're in the know." The reporter shook Caz's hand, and he smiled a polite smile that didn't reach his eyes.

Putting her hand on his arm, the reporter stepped closer. "That was great, Caspian, thank you."

Caz murmured something she couldn't hear.

"Lots of fans are going through what you're going through. With the divorce. It would really help them if you'd open up and share your story. I'd be honored to give you that platform. So you can give back."

Caz didn't respond, just stared at the reporter, his arms crossed over his chest.

The reporter never lost her cool. "Let me know." She turned to the AD. "How about Lorene next?"

The AD's face tensed. "Unfortunately, Lorene's not here, so we'll have to schedule that one later in the week. Petra's here, though. I've sent for her. You can finish up with Caz."

Caz said, "We're done."

The AD clapped his hands together. "I know. Garrett can be your third interview. Garrett."

In response to his name, Garrett trotted over. "You need me?"

"Yeah, can you fill in for Lorene for a brief interview? While we get Petra ready?"

"Sure." A look of dislike crossed Garrett's face as he recognized the reporter.

Caz leaned near him and said in a low tone, "Watch your mouth."

Garrett shoved his big frame into one of the cozy nook chairs. "Or what? You'll kick me off my land and refuse to let me speak Gaelic?"

Caz's lips twitched, but he didn't respond.

Ashley handed Caz a script. "Want to run lines?" She'd never offered before, but it seemed prudent to put a lid on this situation.

Caz took the script, crossed his arms over his chest, and stared at the nook. "Later."

Garrett poured himself a cup of tea and pushed the sugar cubes aside. His expression fell. "No shortbread? No biscuits?"

Karla ignored him and did her intro. "We're here with Garrett Campbell on set of his latest film. Tell us, what's it really like to work with your best friend?"

"Great fun." Garrett dug around the tray and popped a sugar cube in his mouth. The dish was emptying fast.

"Now you can tell us, who's he really seeing? Lorene or Petra?"

Caz stayed focused on the interview.

Garrett relaxed back in the chair and his accent got heavier than normal. "I'm as free as the rain in Scotland."

"All these beautiful actresses on set, and there's no romance going on?"

"'Tis a sad, sad state, and difficult to believe, I know."

The reporter leaned forward and rubbed Garrett's kilt between her fingers. "So, you know me, I have to touch that famous kilt." She growled. "Rough, what's it made of?"

If you looked close enough, you could see the distaste in his mint-green eyes. Garrett said, "Highland heather soaked in the waters of Loch Ness, stolen from the hooves of a Kelpie by a Cailleach Bheur." He settled back further into his chair, forcing the reporter's hand to fall away.

Caz leaned toward Ashley's ear and whispered, "This is a long story. I've heard it before." He nodded his head toward the back exit.

Taking the hint, Ashley followed him out of the warehouse and down the crunchy path to his trailer. Caz unlocked the door and stepped inside. His trailer smelled like the clean, ocean fragrance of his soap. Ashley closed the door behind her.

Red pages of the script flew through the air as Caz flung himself on his couch and put one arm over his eyes. "Ergh, what rubbish."

Ashley perched on the sofa's armrest, silent.

Caz frowned. "Going to spin this? Going to tell me some nice, homespun tale about the Fry Hut? To make that crap interview seem better?"

"No. No. I'm here to console you. How awful was that? You poor thing. Why, I didn't know how you'd bear the interview a moment longer." Ashley let the full force of her talent for sarcasm fly.

Quickly sitting up, Caz snagged her arm and yanked her down on top of him.

"Oomph." His hard chest didn't provide a soft landing.

"I suffered."

Ashley laughed. "I suffered too. I had to hear her." She put her hands against the couch cushion and pushed up.

"Your pain wasn't as deep as mine."

Ashley laughed harder. "But I have to live without knowing."

Caz raised his eyebrows.

"Your favorite color or, more importantly, boxers or briefs, you man beast." Her laughter caused her to collapse against him.

Caz smiled wickedly and put his hands on the top button of his jeans, and unbuttoned them.

Laughing harder, Ashley grabbed his wrist to stop him.

A quick knock sounded on the door. Caz didn't have time to respond as it was immediately flung open.

The AD stood there, his mouth ajar to the point that his goatee touched his chest. Olive hung out next to him with shiny eyes and a prissy grin. "We're looking for Petra." She crooked her head inside and looked around.

The AD yanked her elbow backwards. "Oh, uh, excuse us." The trailer door slammed shut.

The absurdity struck Ashley. She slid off Caz's lap and onto the floor beside the couch, laughing. "That is so not going to play well," Ashley said. "*Unidentified blonde saves Caz from overdose while putting out a fire in his trailer.*"

"*During the birth of their half human baby,*" Caz said, offering her a hand up.

***

The AD paced, glaring at his tablet. Ashley knew why he was mad. Lorene hadn't shown all week. Today, he'd scheduled her to shoot a minor stunt. Because the stunt used special effects, Lorene was supposed to perform it without a stunt double. However, Lorene was not here.

The AD said, "PA."

"Yes?" Olive shoved in front of her. Because Olive stood a half foot shorter, Ashley still had a clear view of the AD's annoyed eyes. He looked from Ashley to Olive with a dismissive gaze, and his eyes landed back on Ashley. "You're about Lorene's height. Get dressed and help." The AD turned to the costume area and yelled with an annoyed edge in his voice, "Cutter, Powder, dress Ashley in Lorene's costume so she can perform the stunt."

"Uh, okay," Ashley said, as if her agreement mattered. She went to makeup first, and Powder did the works: base, lip stain, false eyelashes. Next came the red wig, and last a trip to the costume area, where Cutter handed her a feminine, dreamy sundress with a tight bodice. Over the sundress, he clipped on a suspension harness. The green straps circled her waist and hung over her shoulders like suspenders. At each shoulder and the front and back of her waist hung metal clamps that would attach to wires once she got to the set.

This was Ashley's first visit to the green screen studio. The AD, who'd walked her over, said, "Once you're in place, you'll pull backwards, lift two feet off the ground, then lower to the floor. We'll do the action slowly and make the cut look fast on film." The AD eyed her sundress. "Cutter wants to go with a dress, but we may have to switch to pants if you need a full body harness."

Ashley wasn't worried about the harness; she just hoped the dress didn't fly up. She moved onto the center stage and a stunt coordinator's assistant joined her.

"The cameraman will film you in front of this green screen. Later we'll digitally remove the ropes, straps, and wires, then edit in background shots of an exploding car." He explained each detail as he hooked her up to the wires. "Walk forward and when you hit your mark, we'll lift you up backwards and down."

"Picture is up."

Next, she heard some information about the shot, "Roll camera," and then "Speed."

The clapper guy called out, "Marker" and clicked the clapperboard shut.

"Action."

Ashley took a step forward.

"One."

Ashley neared the mark. Suddenly the harness jerked and lifted her backwards into the air. The straps dug into her waist, pressing the little pearl buttons that ran along the front of her sundress into her skin. Once in the air, the harness suspended her there for a few minutes then lowered her to the ground, where she lay flat out.

"Cut."

"Good, good expression. The shock then the pain was perfect. Let's go again."

Grabbing hold of the green wires, Ashley pulled up. When she was upright, Powder got beside her, touched up her makeup, and ran a hairbrush through parts of the red wig. During each touchup, Powder described a trapeze artist she used to date.

Ashley performed the stunt several times and the lying AD never went on the count of three. She couldn't blame him, though; if she knew the lift was coming she'd tense and not give him the right expression.

Appearing to be in pain became easier with each take. The straps hurt and she hoped the filming would end soon. The restraints had become creepy and the waist kept tightening, threatening to cut off her ability to breathe.

"Okay, good job, that's a wrap," the AD said. "Powder, they need you on stage B."

Powder waved and headed out.

Ashley smiled and tilted her head against the strap, relieved. She'd needed a break but hadn't wanted to ask. This experience would make it much harder for her to mock actors in the future; some of their work was hard, and she definitely understood why Petra refused to do wirework. The stunt coordinators were ruthless.

She hung from the air while the wire guy did something technical over by the wall. The harness jolted, digging the pearl buttons deeper. Torn between the desire to screech at the technician to get her down and the desire to not sound like a diva, Ashley didn't know what to do. She wiggled and tried to shift the strap that pinched the most.

The pain lessened when she used her arms to pull her weight up, but her arms weren't strong enough to hold the pose consistently. She'd opened her mouth to give in and call the technician for help when Caz walked on set. *Thank God*. "Caz, come here."

After murmuring something to another actor, Caz joined her. He eyed the equipment. "So this is where you've been. I was shooting with Petra, and I asked, but no one knew."

"This thing hurts. See if you can move the strap or unhook the clasp."

"Where?"

"Waist, that claw thingy and those pointy buttons."

Caz slid a hand under the metal clasp and Ashley felt instant relief. She groaned. "Thanks."

He frowned and jerked at the clasp, but the belt didn't unlatch. One arm slid under the back of her thighs and he held her against him. The new position took all the weight off her waist. *Heaven*. "Ohhh, thanks." Ashley lowered her hands to his shoulders and flexed her fingers against them. "Thank you, thank you. This makes up for all your random errands."

Caz fiddled at the claw.

Ashley poked at one of the pearl buttons. "It's these stupid buttons. Cutter will have to change them out for Lorene." Tucking two fingers into the gap between buttons at her waist, Caz pulled the fabric apart. One button pinged to the floor.

He stared a moment, then yelled at the stunt coordinator who was jotting notes. "Get my assistant down, now."

For once, she didn't mind being called his assistant; not when his demands got someone to leap up and help her. Wanting to be free, she also didn't correct Caz by pointing out that the coordinator had assistants who did tasks like latching and unlatching.

The stunt coordinator said, "Sure thing." With a few jerks of his hands, the harness released and she fell against Caz. The straps dropped, dragged down by the clasps. They clanked against the floor.

"Oh, good."

Caz lowered her to her feet.

"About the chase scene —" the stunt coordinator said.

"I need a minute." Caz led Ashley to the side of the set. He hooked a finger in the waist of her dress and parted the fabric.

Ashley looked down curiously. Her skin had livid red marks from the straps, and small scratches from the pearl buttons. She'd be bruised tomorrow.

Caz brushed over the spot with his index finger. "Why didn't you say something?"

Ashley shrugged and sucked in her abdomen in response to the electric sensation caused by his touch. Her reaction had nothing to do with pain.

A crew member called from across the set, "Hey, Caz, you ready?"

"Your turn," Ashley said. Caz nodded, and she was sorry when he withdrew his fingers. She folded her arms over her waist and watched as they put him in a car suspended on a metal frame, the green screen behind him. His hands gripped the wheel and his expression became tense as he checked the mirrors and spoke in a cell phone. The mood intensified, and he shifted and jerked the wheel.

Caz was an amazing actor, exciting. Ashley had no doubt that his fake expressions were better than her real ones. Were all actors good at being expressive or did they actually feel things more intensely? She put her back against the wall and lowered herself to the floor so she could see the rest of the scene.

***

Shooting required careful camera positioning, microphone placement, and lighting adjustments. Today's scene was set in a police headquarters, so they fitted the stage with desks, mug shots, and a number of extras.

Lorene's character, Aurora, would drop by to see her true love at work. Caz's reaction to Aurora would expose his weakness in front of the villain, giving him the idea of how to destroy Caz's character—harm Aurora.

The AD paced and glared at his computer tablet, his nose close to the screen. Lorene hadn't shown up. "Ash, get in costume so we can shoot this."

Ashley's head tilted and her mouth opened. Then she shook her head no.

The AD didn't care. "Sit and wait for Caz then bring him a cup of tea. I've seen you do that every day, so I know you can handle it." His words were slow and his tone was patronizing.

Ashley felt her face flush and palms sweat. She didn't want to, but everyone was looking at her, and there were so many people standing around, ready to go. She swallowed and nodded. Powder and Cutter got her dressed in record time and she wished it had taken them longer. Taking a deep breath, she sat down and stared at the extras while winding her fingers together. Cutter had kitted them out like the dregs of society and they seemed quite comfortable with the role.

"Take your notebook." Powder held it out. Her purple painted lips matched her nails today.

Ashley was grateful for the idea. She'd hyperventilate if she had to sit in the fake waiting room with nothing to do except think about how stupid she looked. Opening the familiar book, she propped the back against the torn card table and sketched. Time spent drawing was her favorite time of the day, so she relaxed, quite happy to wait as long as necessary, though the wig was hot under the lights, and she'd be happier when she could remove it until they were ready for her.

The table jerked, making her pencil skid across the page.

Ashley said, "Earthquake," and slid under the desk.

CHAPTER 9

The nearby crew and cast laughed.

Boomer said, "False alarm, Texas. I added a table and accidently hit your desk."

Olive arrived back in time to witness Ashley's fear. Hands tucked into her new black overalls, she laughed longer and louder than any of the others. Ashley could see their mirth clearly from her position under the desk, but she couldn't think of anything to say.

Caz put a hand on the edge and leaned down with a smile. "You can come out now."

She didn't know what he saw on her face, but his smile faded and he straightened. "I need a break."

The AD said, "Take fifteen, everybody."

Caz leaned down and offered his hand. "Walk with me to the tea kiosk." Ashley didn't move for a second. Caz said in a low voice only she could hear, "Come with me, Ashley." She took his hand and let him pull her out.

Cutter came over. "What about the—?"

Caz said, "Not now, I need a break."

Instead of the tea kiosk, he led her out the back door to his trailer.

Ashley sat on his sofa and curled her hands around her knees. "Sorry, I—" Her voice trailed off, and she heard him moving around the kitchenette. Water streamed from the faucet. China clinked against a tray. Minutes later Caz arrived with tea on a full service tray.

He poured a cup of the hot brew, added sugar and milk, and put the warm cup in her hands. "Drink."

Ashley wanted to apologize, say she was fine and being silly. Instead, she sipped the bracing tea. After a minute, she felt better, and with that came the rush of embarrassment. “Sorry, I didn’t realize they hit the table. I was just keyed up.”

Caz shrugged and drank his tea. “So you don’t like earthquakes. It’s not the stupidest fear to have.”

“They bother you?”

“I’ve never been in one, but I’m sure it would.”

He looked so calm, she doubted it. Ashley drank the rest of her tea then fiddled with the porcelain.

Caz put a script in her hands. “I’ll read the lines. You read Lorene’s part with me?”

“Okay.”

They hung out longer than fifteen minutes and Ashley relaxed as they practiced.

She felt more confident and only a little embarrassed by the time they returned to take their places.

The AD said, “Places. Picture is up. Roll camera. Speed.”

“Marker.” The clapper man clicked the clapperboard shut.

“Action.”

Ashley set her notebook down and walked over to where Caz sat at a fake desk, stopping on her mark, feeling stupid and awkward. She held out the cup. Caz put his hand over hers and brushed his thumb over the back. Ashley’s shoulders relaxed; she smiled.

“Cut. Got it.”

***

Petra held the latest tabloid in her ringed fingers, scouring the pages. “Where am I? Where am I?” She made a delighted squeal and swung the glossy image toward the onlookers. A sizable shot of a bikini-clad Petra on the beach experiencing a wardrobe malfunction flashed them. Petra flipped to the next page. She frowned and pursed her lips.

Caz had made the tabloid also, with a picture taken from the doorway of his trailer. The picture contained a girl with blonde hair leaning over a smiling Caz. His hands rested on the fly of his unbuttoned jeans. Someone must have been behind Olive and the AD with a camera.

Petra read the caption aloud. “Caz and his mysterious blonde companion take time off on the set of *Eternal Loss, Eternal Revenge*.” Petra narrowed her eyes and stared harder at the picture.

Powder turned with raised eyebrows. Ashley widened her eyes innocently and stepped forward to fake interest in the photo. Her shoulders relaxed when she got a closer look. She felt enormous gratitude for her long hair. Its messy length obscured her features just as it had in the limo.

Dad didn't even like her going out with guys who picked her up at the front door and met him. He'd be furious to see her featured in a tabloid, especially while rolling around on top of a couch with a guy—then throw in the fact that he was an actor: Armageddon.

Petra tossed the magazine aside, exchanging it for her laptop. After going online, she typed with the tips of her nails. *Click, click.*

The *Tween In 'Trinity of Stars'* interview downloaded. In addition to the chopped-up and spliced Q&A, the reporter gave a brief wrap-up. "My *Trinity of Stars* interview almost turned into a Duo of Stars. Where is the missing Lorene? Well, you didn't hear it here, but buzz on the set says poor Lorene can't face being around the power couple Caspian and Petra. Or, as we call them, CasPet. So what do you think, viewers? CasPet or are you holding out for CasLore? Vote on our website."

Olive said, "CasPet."

Petra grinned and clicked on another news link. This one featured Caz's impromptu signature signing at the tea shack. Nine times out of ten, studio regulars and out-of-state tourists filled the tea shack, but not that day. Caz had happened to greet the tour on a day that a member of the press was visiting incognito with his family. Caz's joke about needing tea, which had gone over well with the kiosk crowd, played just as well when repeated on national television.

Petra flicked through some more screens. "I need to interact more with my fans. I should upload more news about my day. What I'm doing, where we are with the filming. They'd love that."

"They would," Olive said.

***

"Let me see it." Caz put down the book he was reading.

Ashley checked out the cover: *Le Misanthrope ou l'Atrabilaire amoureux*. "*The Misanthrope.* I'm reading that too, for school."

Caz nodded. "Let me see."

"Huh?"

He lifted the hem of her T-shirt. Ashley looked around quickly, but no one was watching, so she let him. Several splotchy purple bruises marred the skin around her waist. He frowned and ran the back of his hand along them. "Do they hurt?"

Ashley didn't answer, distracted by the sensation caused by his hand.

No, it didn't hurt. She didn't know what he saw in her eyes, but he smiled and slid his warm palm around her back. Pulling her closer, he leaned forward to murmur in her ear about the movies playing at a nearby theater.

"What are you guys doing?" Petra asked. "I was going to tell you about my new armlet."

Caz looked at Petra in annoyance, and it took a moment for Ashley to snap out of the fuzzy sensation that had ensnared her. When her head cleared, she deliberately stepped away from Caz, frowning at him in confusion. What was he doing? What was she letting him do?

Caz said, "We were talking about what movie we're going to see tonight."

Petra blew out a breath.

Ashley felt torn, confused. Olive chose that moment to join them. She dragged a large laundry bag overflowing with envelopes behind her, and pushed the bulk against Ashley's leg. "You're going to have to help with this fan mail like the rest of us. You have to do your share of the work. I'm not going to ask again."

Ashley had never seen the bag. She lifted an envelope and peeped inside. "Snail mail?"

"Fan mail."

"Sorry, Caz, looks like I'll be busy tonight with this." Ashley tipped the envelope to the side and a slim piece of elasticized fabric fell out. They all looked down at the red lace thong. Ashley read, "Dear Caspian…"

***

"Who's that?" Ashley asked Petra and pointed to a military-looking man dressed in loose black pants and tight black T-shirt. He was talking to Caz and his agent.

"Trainer. Nice ass. Tight abs." Powder lined up her makeup brushes. "Where is number four? Olive better not have been in here again." Her eyes took on a militant gleam that was in contrast to today's bohemian dress.

"Trainer for what?"

"Caz's next film. He's going to be doing some martial arts training on his off-time."

"Caz barely has any off-time."

Powder shrugged.

Ashley walked over, blatantly eavesdropping.

Caz said to his agent, "If they want to start early, I can train in September during postproduction."

"You've committed to this movie and a lot of people depend on you making it happen." His agent crossed her arms over her chest and sent a longing look at the coffee cart.

"I said I'd do the movie."

"Well, doing the movie means working on other people's timelines, not just yours. They need you to do this."

Caz frowned, his mouth tight.

The AD said, "People, gather round."

Ashley joined the rest of the crew and cast. The AD said, "The director has read the recent press, and he requires me to make a formal announcement regarding cast hook-ups."

The crew laughed.

The AD said, "There are to be none." He finished his command and stroked his little goatee. He'd gotten the ends trimmed about an inch.

Several people turned to stare at Ashley, which she found offensive. She hadn't had a date or even been kissed by any member of the movie crew. Their stares were so unfair.

Petra giggled wildly and tapped her index finger, heavy with layered rings, against Caz's arm. "Okay, we'll stop."

Caz frowned and moved away from her, crossing his arms over his chest.

Powder ran a hand over her hair and looked back at someone in the crowd. Ashley followed her gaze. Four men stood behind her. Ashley couldn't tell which one was Powder's secret boyfriend. None wore a monitored ankle bracelet or any suspicious makeup smears. Surely, someone trysting with the makeup artist would have at least a lipstick smudge on his collar or a stray smear of mascara.

Petra's need for attention interrupted Ashley's investigation. She raised her hands straight in the air and clapped them. "Don't forget my party tonight. The bash will be a blow-out. See you there." Her eyelash extensions made a big wink. "And no hooking up." The crowd laughed.

Powder turned to Ashley. "I'll see you at her party tonight?"

Ashley wrinkled her nose.

At her expression, Powder said, "The party's for the whole crew. You're going."

"What are you wearing?"

"Feathers and teal makeup. Teal streaks in my hair if we break early enough tonight. Or maybe orange. You?"

Ashley looked down at her jeans and T-shirt. "Um."

"Don't," Powder said. "You show up like that and I'll take you to the car and redo your outfit and makeup with a pair of scissors and ebony night eyeliner."

Ashley smiled, fully intending to wear something other than her usual jeans. "You'll have to wait and see."

***

Ash could hear music through the door of Petra's apartment. She raised a painted pink nail and pressed the doorbell, wondering what Powder would think of her outfit. She wore a pink spaghetti-strapped top, black miniskirt, and black flats. Her makeup up was light except her eyes, which were smoky.

The stunt coordinator waved her in. The loft smelled a lot like Petra's trailer, but the perfume wasn't as overwhelming here in the larger space.

About thirty people stood inside, most of whom she knew. Glancing beyond them, she drew in a breath at the décor. Every wall glowed a different neon color, and against every color hung a dark-framed artistic shot of Petra. The images were completed in all mediums, oils, watercolors, charcoal, and film. When she tore her gaze from the ego extravaganza, she saw Cutter.

He wore a gold top loose over shiny gold skinny jeans. His brown hair was thick with mousse and stood straight up. Cutter eyed her up and down with a hand clasped to his mouth. "O.M.G., it's like you're a girl. Who knew?"

"So says the guy wearing eyeliner. Where are—"

Cutter moved past her to greet someone else.

The eyes in the portrait hung on the lemon wall seemed to follow her steps. Creepy. The doorbell chimed and more people flowed in. Ashley spotted a wave, and was happy to see Powder. She was dressed in an orange leather jumpsuit and stood talking to a short, sturdy-looking guy in a pastel, button-down collar shirt over in the corner. What was his name? Ashley couldn't remember, but it had something to do with sound. He worked in one of the offices.

Heading in their direction, she took a glass from one of the circulating waiters, and sipped the pale gold liquid infused with fizzy bubbles. Mid-path she ran into Petra holding court. "Hi, Petra, thanks for inviting me."

Petra stared to the left and right of her, as if trying to see if Ashley brought a date. Spotting Ashley alone, she waved a dismissive hand weighed down by a sparkling emerald ring that matched her large emerald earrings. "Yeah, have fun." She turned her focus back to her minions to continue her story. "I sat there."

Olive said, "You're kidding."

"For at least an hour, in that wooden chair with its straight back."

Olive covered her mouth with her hand. "No way."

"Exactly. Only my dance training kept me sane. Having to hold my posture that long. You can't imagine."

Olive's jaw dropped. "You know ballet?"

"Oh yes, I've studied all kinds of dance."

Ashley left their group and continued toward her friend. She greeted Powder with a hug and the guy with a wave. Then she tried to be subtle about attempting to identify Powder's date. She peered through the crowd. There were no chain-wearers in sight.

"Hey, I was about to tell Jason here about the kissing pentagon or maybe show him."

Ashley's eyes widened and her head swung back to pastel shirt. Jason? Powder was dating a guy who favored pastel and dressed like an accountant? Sipping her drink, she flushed a little and didn't know what to say.

"Is the technique so secret only the Pentagon knows?" Jason's gaze focused on Powder's orange lipstick. He seemed half-scared and half-eager.

Powder smiled. "Probably, but that's not what the name means." She looked at Ashley. "Come on, architect, what's pentagon mean?"

"Five-sided?"

"Right." Powder proceeded to detail the five-step plan.

Ashley was embarrassed, but she totally wanted to know, so she stayed glued to her spot, trying to contain her amusement during the rendition.

When the waiter came by with a drink tray, Powder scooped off three martini glasses and passed them out. Ashley took one, placing her empty champagne flute on the tray. She'd totally have to catch a ride with someone. Putting her lips to the cold rim, she tried the drink. The concoction tasted like bitter, dry Sprite laced with orange juice and cough syrup. Ashley took another sip.

Powder smiled at Jason and put a mango-orange fingernail against her cheek. Jason took a deep drink, his eyes still on Powder. "That is the hottest thing I've ever heard."

Caz walked up in the middle of Jason's sentence and took the martini from Ashley's hand. He took a sip. "What's hot?"

Ashley straightened and didn't answer.

"The pentagon," Jason said with reverence. "Powder and I have to be somewhere." He took Powder's hand and led her away with an intent expression.

"Ta," Powder said, not hiding her smirk.

Ashley shook her head. She guessed the technique didn't even have to be perfected to capture a guy, just vocalized. What 'til Marissa heard. She'd totally try it out. Ashley wasn't that gutsy. Her fingers flexed. Empty-handed, she turned to Caz. "We're not on set, why do you get to take my drink? It's not very gentlemanly."

Caz lifted the cold crystal to her lips, offering her a sip, and the cool drink filled her mouth. The move was kind of hot.

He said, "What was the pentagon—"

Petra's embrace cut off the rest of his sentence, and the jolt caused the gold liquid to slosh toward the rim of the glass.

Ashley wiped the wet spill off her chin and backed up a step.

"I am so glad you came," Petra said. "I knew you would."

This close, Petra's perfume filled the air. She must have spritzed on some more because the fragrance was like her trailer—eau d' overwhelming. Ashley brushed at the end of her nose.

A new pop song came on, causing Petra to sway her perfect body in time with the beat, bumping into Caz.

He stepped away. "Thank you for the invitation."

"Well, I work so hard. So do you. Our roles are so important. I knew we'd need a break. Have you tried my passion Petra punch yet? The recipe was created specifically for me."

Caz opened his mouth to reply but the beautiful Petra kept talking. "The recipe calls for vermouth, champagne, schnapps, oh, everything. The taste explosion will blow your mind." Petra laughed. "I mean, literally blow your mind. You wore gray." Petra crumpled the fabric of his shirt in her fingers. "Gray's my favorite on you, and we totally match." She ran a finger down the faint gray stripe in her blouse all the way to the hem then placed her hand on her small waist, pulling the shirt in even tighter.

Ashley took another slow step backwards. Their clothes didn't match and Caz looked better in blue. If she'd ever wondered what the popular kids talked about, she now knew—themselves. As fascinating as the moment was for them, she preferred to leave. One more step and she could make a discreet turn. Fingers clasped her hand, stilling her.

What was Caz doing? She wasn't on duty. He'd have to save himself from this one. Ashley was about to yank her hand away when she felt his thumb rub against the center of her palm. Her hand trembled in reaction and her fingers clenched around his.

"So after I left the set today," Petra said, "I had so much to do, manicure, pedicure, hair. All day, so…"

Their hands were drawn, attracting attention from those nearby, from everyone but the oblivious Petra, who continued her monologue punctuated by less than subtle touches of Caz's chest. Ashley pulled away again, but Caz's fingers tightened, not releasing her.

Ashley whispered, "Let go."

"Yes," Caz said. "I told Boomer we'd be right over."

Petra frowned and she noticed their linked hands for the first time. The silence was a blessed respite from her chattering. It didn't last long.

Petra's jaw dropped; then she recovered with a high laugh. "Yes, let's see what Boomer's up to."

Boomer sat on the floor in the corner, a deck of cards, a pair of dice, and a stack of spoons beside his leg. "I'm trying to get a game going, but no one's ready for the spoon-a-thon."

They were in Hollywood, so they probably thought he was melting drugs on the spoons. Ashley knew he wasn't a user, so she knelt down, folding her knees to the side to keep her skirt at a decent angle, and reached for the cards. "What are we playing?" The thin cards flipped against her fingertips as she shuffled.

"Spoons."

Caz sat beside her. "Deal me in."

Caz's presence was enough to enlarge the group to ten. And the spoon-a-thon began.

Olive took a center seat. Unless the turn was her deal, she never paid attention to the cards. She hovered on her knees, eyes on the spoons, ready to grab one. Her strategy wasn't bad for someone so short.

Petra was out after the first round. After four rounds, Ashley and Caz were both out and it was Cutter's deal.

"Get out of here with me?" Caz asked in her ear.

She did need a lift home. Ashley put her drink on an end table. "Okay."

Caz led her across the thick carpet and out the front. Through the darkness, she recognized his Jaguar limo, the same one from the airport. He must have called the driver because the car wasn't far from the entrance. They walked straight for it.

A couple of fans and paparazzi stood near, under a streetlight. One fan stripped off her *I love Caspian* T-shirt and swung the cotton overhead like a rally towel while screaming, "Caspian."

Another raised her head and howled at the moon. "He's here."

Ashley's eyes widened at their enthusiasm. With a lowered head, she quickly opened the limo door and slid inside, melting into the leather seat.

Caz slammed the door on the fan girls. "Sorry we had to leave early. There were a lot of mobile cell phones out."

"I saw some." Ashley peeped out of the back tinted window. Flashes lit up the night, and his fans slapped the trunk of the limo.

"There's only so much I want to be portrayed partying on YouTube."

"It was just spoons."

"The tabloids will doctor the photos."

Ashley nodded. He was right. Whatever he did at that party would end up online, accessible forever. “Not cool.”

“Exactly.”

“I’m not ready to go home. I had a drink. And my dad will be able to tell.” Not that he’d be home, but this would be the one time he made it in before her.

“We could hang out in my trailer.”

What a line. “And read more of your fan mail? No thanks.”

Caz reached a hand toward the door of the minibar. “Want to drive along the coast?”

“Yes.” Ashley bounced against the Jaguar’s gray seat. “Great view and neither of us has to drive.”

The coast lay outside the right window. The spectacular view sitting beside her captured her attention even more. She shifted against the leather cushion.

The driver’s voice came through the speaker. “I know a semi-private beach, if you guys want to get out for a bit.”

Caz looked at Ashley. When she nodded, he flipped the switch on the intercom. “Yeah, thanks.”

Not much later, the driver parked the limo at the edge of a sandy path; street lamps lit the trail with a circular glow every ten feet or so. “The pavement drops off about ten feet from the water.”

“Thanks.” She toed off her flats and Caz kicked off his topsiders. After rolling the hem of his pants, he took her hand and led her down the path.

Concrete brushed with sand turned to wooden planks. The sand shifted with each step, falling through the space between the planks. Then the walkway dropped away altogether and there was only loose and gritty sand under her feet until they reached the water’s edge. “The water is colder and clearer here than the Gulf of Mexico. But I still love Galveston.” Ashley tapped her foot against the packed wet sand, enjoying the sensation on the soles of her feet. “What’s an English beach like?”

“Colder than California and Texas. Cliffs. Different, but waves crash, and the salty fish smell’s the same.”

“So do you think you’ll do this forever?” Ashley waved in the air, so he’d know she meant the whole Hollywood thing.

“Can’t tell with this industry,” Caz said. “Popularity fades and careers end just like that.”

“Oh. No. You have one of those deep, rich voices. Actors with voices like yours have long careers if they want them. Plus, you’re exceptionally talented.”

"Thanks." Caz sounded surprised. "You're not usually so full of praise. Is it the champagne? If it was I can ask the driver to stop and purchase a case."

Ashley laughed and rolled her eyes. "You don't need my praise. You hear compliments all day from people who know what they're talking about." She looked out at distant lights on a ship. "You could do something else. Chuck all the fame and go to college?"

He kind of laughed in response.

"No really, why not? I mean, you're great at the acting bit but you don't seem to like the press part. They're both important."

"Since I was fourteen and my first indie film became a cult classic, no one has suggested I quit. Not once."

Ashley rubbed her toe in the sand, admiring the pink polish against the beige granules. She dug a small trail. "I'm not suggesting you quit either. I just wondered. Plus, I've seen you reading literature; French literature. That would be interesting to study."

"I like the characters. They're different and fascinating. What they teach me enriches my roles."

"So, no going off to college with me next year?" Ashley asked half in jest, feeling a little empty.

"I've thought about university but can't get the time off." He stared back up the hill. "The studio's lined up years of projects and they're pushing me to commit."

Ashley nodded. She didn't really know what to say. A lot of jobs depended on his acting. He brought in money. She'd heard that more than once while on set. She brushed her fingertips along his high cheekbones, near the dark circles she'd noticed under his eyes. "You look tired. How early do you get up for those martial arts sessions?"

"I'm fine."

She stilled her hand. "What about a holiday?"

His voice brightened then dimmed. "I'd love one, but my agent says time off won't work out production-wise. She calls it striking while the iron is hot."

Ashley rolled her eyes. "So what if the heat cools some? You could still be successful with less crazed attention. Or, again, so what if the fame ended? You could do other stuff."

Caz didn't respond.

"When was your last real break?"

"For any real length of time? It was before I was fourteen, a trip to the continent, but the schedule's fine. I'm fine." Caz pointed up the beach. "Want to walk along the edge?"

"Nah, I'm going to sit over there and listen to the surf." Ashley waved toward a bench near the path. "You go ahead."

Caz dropped his arm around her shoulders. "I'll go with you." They trudged up the sandy incline to the bench. His arm slid from her shoulders to her waist. On the bench, he pulled her close, his left arm around her waist, his right going up to cup her face. His head angled toward hers.

The bright white light flashed, illuminating the night. Ashley tucked her face against Caz's shoulder. Caz stood, his arm around her, tucking her against his side, shielding her from the camera.

The photographer, talking beneath the huge lens of a professional camera, said, "Evening, Mr. Thaymore, who's your date? Does Petra know you're cheating on her?"

Caz stiffened but ignored the reporter's taunts. He grabbed her hand and they ran, as quick as the shifting sand would permit, back to the safety of the limo.

Chapter 10

The love scene drew a large crowd. Ashley had read that they usually took place on a closed set in order to be sensitive to the actors. That wasn't the case in warehouse 47. Petra Pelinski wasn't a sensitive type of person. She'd walked around in red lingerie for two days now and seemed to prefer a large crowd.

Ashley had planned to skip out before they started shooting. She didn't want to see Caz kiss Petra even though they were just acting.

His character had two sex scenes in the movie. One with Petra, whose character was a vixen about to betray him: a hook-up that was supposed to be rough and exciting. That moment would serve as a direct contrast with the tender scene he'd shoot with Lorene. The sex scene with Lorene would be filmed in candlelight in a floating, dreamy sequence. Memories of their romance would haunt his character throughout the film—his one true love killed because of the case he was investigating.

Lorene hadn't shown up for work yet. The executives were getting anxious, according to Powder. The rumor mill said Lorene was jockeying for a larger paycheck. Recently, Lorene had spoken to the press about being unhappy with her role and with the script in general. Powder explained that those tactics were a way of negotiating for more money or a bigger part in a future film. When the studio gave in, Lorene would praise the film and the size of her role as loudly as anyone would listen. It was a tried and true Hollywood move.

The director adjusted a camera, then addressed Petra and Caz. "I want to see heat and passion between the vixen and the hero. Show me fire."

Ashley jerked at the heavy cable. She didn't want to watch Caz and Petra go for fire. She wanted to tack down this cable and leave. The cable resisted her pull, so she wiggled the end. How did these things get so entwined when they were just lying there? This was like dealing with necklaces in a jewelry box, if the necklaces weighed ten pounds each.

"They look so great together," Olive said in an aside to Ashley. "So natural. I'm sure they're really a couple and are keeping the romance secret." Olive didn't try to help adjust the cables. "I'm not supposed to say anything, but I can tell."

Ashley looked between Caz and Petra. She couldn't see the love. She yanked again.

The AD said, "Picture is up."

Ashley knew she had to get out of there. She had to adjust this one last piece—tug, turn, shove. Ergh, how had it hooked in with the black one?

"Roll sound."

Crap. That meant sound recording had started. She had to stay.

Next, someone gave information about the take, "Sound speed, roll camera," then "Speed." The clapper guy called out, "Marker." *Click*. The clapperboard shut. "Action."

Don't look, Ashley told herself.

Caz's character entered the room and found Petra's character beside the bed in a negligee.

Ashley watched. She couldn't help it.

Caz pulled his shirt from the waistband of his trousers while staring at the vixen. Loosening his buckle, he slipped his belt free and dropped it. His expression was angry and suspicious. Next, he jerked at the buttons on his shirt and yanked it off. Petra writhed on the bed while Caz undressed.

Ashley watched with a frown. People were right. When a love scene wasn't on the big screen, and didn't have music, the act didn't look romantic at all. He seemed unhappy and Petra's movements came off weird, like she was having a seizure.

A shirtless Caz leaned over Petra. Now that view was worth the price of a ticket. His hands were on either side of her head and only his lips touched her when they kissed. His head didn't move much. Petra's arms flew out beside her on the bed and she gyrated again, trying to keep as much of her body in the shot as possible.

"Cut."

Immediately, Caz pulled back and looked at the director.

"That was super hot," Olive said.

Ashley shot her a disbelieving look. If you're going to suck up, at least praise something that was good, like Caz without a shirt, *wow.*

"Let's wrap for today," the director said.

Ashley sighed, sorry to hear that. She knew they hadn't gotten the shot, so that meant tomorrow would be day three of Petra wearing only a negligee and a toe ring. She tugged on the cable, and now that the urgency had been eliminated, it dropped right into place. Ashley kicked the compliant rope and stepped away.

The director huffed out a sigh, rubbed a hand across his forehead, and closed his eyes. Opening them, he said, "Writing, leads, let's go look at the dailies." The director caught sight of Ashley. "Bring coffee."

***

This was her first time in the viewing room. The miniature theater had about twenty seats, a large screen; and it was the first one she'd been in that didn't smell like popcorn. The lights dimmed and an image appeared, cued up to the bedroom scene. Frozen on screen, Caz and Petra appeared beautiful together, like something out of a high-end cologne advertisement.

Tomorrow when he rolled around on the sheets, she planned to ask him to whisper the name of some fancy perfume, in an intent rush, just to make her laugh. Ashley passed out coffee while the team discussed the short soundless scene. When the clips ended, the lights rose.

"Opinions," the director said.

The AD stared at his computer tablet and poised his fingers above the screen to record notes.

Caz said, "My character wouldn't sleep with her."

"I know what guys are like," Petra said. "Your character's a guy. I'm a super hot vixen, so he'd sleep with me. In fact, I'm surprised the sex doesn't happen more often throughout the script. When I was in —"

"At this point in the investigation, he suspects her of killing his true love," Caz said. "He wouldn't do it."

"This scene got moved," the screenwriter said. "It's not my fault the sex now falls at the end of the investigation. It was supposed to happen earlier."

The director looked at Ashley. "You're part of our target audience. Opinion."

Surprised at being asked, Ashley tilted her head and assessed the image again. "Well, Caz looks great with his shirt off, so it'd be a shame to lose that scene, but that kiss was so not hot."

"I wrote the scene hot." The writer sounded defensive.

The director nodded. "PA, go to Research and ask them for some romantic DVDs. Mark the scenes and get them to Caspian tomorrow." The director turned to the AD, who made notes. "We'll shoot the car chase next instead, rework the schedule." The director turned to Caz.

"Watch the DVDs and we'll reshoot Thursday. I'll make a decision then."

"The PA will help me with the scene?" Caz said, in a way that wasn't really a question.

"Yes." Turning to Ashley, the director commanded, "Show Caspian how to kiss."

CHAPTER 11

Slipping out of the viewing room, Ashley rubbed her hands over her arms and walked down the hall. The outrage on Caz's face had been funny, *but show Caz how to kiss?* Was the director kidding? She bet no one over at the Fry Hut was being asked to give kissing lessons as part of their job. Then again, Marissa did have a pervy new manager while Irina was on her big Italian vacation.

Caz caught up to her halfway down the hall. "What time do you want to come over tomorrow?"

Continuing down the empty corridor, Ashley rubbed her arms again and without looking at him, said, "Mmm, I don't know."

Caz put a hand on her arm to still her. "Why are you so reluctant? It's just a kiss."

Ashley leaned against the wall. His hand remained on her arm and she said, "I know." She shrugged then met his gaze. "I don't know. I'm not an actress, so I guess I just like the thought that if a guy is going to kiss me, it's me he's kissing."

Caz let go of her arm and slid his hand around to the back of her waist. Her eyes flew up to his. Threading his other hand through the back of her hair, Caz leaned forward, close enough that she could smell his cologne, and whispered, "Thanks for helping me, Ashley." Then he tilted his head and lightly kissed her mouth.

Caz's lips were warm and gentle and then gone.

Ashley relaxed against the wall and she smiled up at him. He was right. This would be fine. "Yeah, I'll bring dinner." She winked at him. "You're not a lost cause. You can probably be taught how to kiss." She straightened away from the wall and moved to leave.

Caz tightened his grip in her hair, stilling her. His eyes brightened with intent and his mouth lowered again. This kiss was firmer. His mouth parted hers. She could taste him, tea and warmth and something decidedly Caz. His jaw was rough against her soft skin, exciting.

She moved her hands to the back of his head and lifted to her tiptoes so she could press closer. Her knees weakened, and he moved her back against the wall. Following her, he leaned his body into hers. Teeth, tongue, lips moved, draining her of all thoughts. Her right hand slid down his back, feeling the unyielding muscles she admired. Her left hand threaded into his silky hair.

His fingers slid under the back of her T-shirt and rubbed lightly at the skin of her waist. She made a muffled sound against his mouth and pressed closer. The sensations were amazing, wicked. She bit down lightly on his bottom lip then soothed it with her tongue. Vaguely in the back of her head, she heard the screening door open, but the information didn't stop her from kissing Caz. She didn't stop until she heard the director's praise.

"Much better."

***

Caz tilted his head and stared with an intent expression as Ashley chopped and threw the ingredients together.

"This is TexMex, not California-style Mexican. Like we talked about." Chop, toss, and bake. "It's way better." Ashley served the food on off-white plates she found in his kitchen and they carried them over to his coffee table.

From the first bite forward, his expression was gratifying. He ate everything she put in front of him.

She took a sip of her iced tea. She hadn't bothered to call Dad. His own project kept him horribly busy. Five dinners in a row with him not showing, she'd given up on sharing meals.

"This is good."

"I'm glad you like it."

"Yes. The flavors make me think of holiday."

"Yeah? Have you decided to take one when the shooting wraps?"

Caz shrugged. "My agent is pushing for another film after the press tour."

"That martial arts thing?"

"No, that's a done deal. I mean, one after that."

"Is it a film you're interested in?"

"No, I'm interested in a film based on a Moliere novel, but she's pushing to go big budget."

"Nothing's wrong with low budget. We're studying Moliere too. He's one of the authors on my summer reading list. Just think, if you make the movie, no student will ever have to read the novel again."

"My contribution to education." Caz took another bite, swallowed, and said, "I really want the holiday."

"Well, you've decided then, vacation it is."

"My schedule's not that simple."

Ashley shrugged and moved over to her bag and pulled out five DVDs. It sounded simple to her. "In addition to dinner, I brought the five greatest onscreen movie kisses ever. Prepare to learn."

Caz frowned and took a last bite, carrying his plate back into the kitchen. The plate clattered into the sink. "I know how to kiss."

Ashley laughed. "We can watch these tomorrow if you want." She put the movies on his coffee table. Shouldering her bag, she headed to the door. "I marked the scene numbers on the covers, so you can fast forward right to the good stuff."

"I didn't mean you should leave." Caz moved around the kitchenette. He tugged her toward the couch and put her drink back in her hand. "You said you'd help." He frowned as the ice clinked against the side of her glass, and he gave a small shudder. "Iced tea."

"If you'd try it, you might like it." After putting her bag down by the sofa, she took a sip of the icy drink.

"Never." Caz sounded resolute, as if she'd suggested he commit a felony. He moved to the player and slid the top DVD in.

She caught the remote control he threw to her. "This is so, uh, weird. I bet Petra would be glad to help you."

His mouth twisted, and he thrummed his fingers against the couch cushion, shaking his head at her suggestion. He poured himself another cup of hot tea.

Ashley scooted a bit away from him to lessen the tension. Kicking off her shoes, she folded her legs beneath her. "Have you done this a lot? Screen kisses?"

"I had a small part in a French film not too long ago. So yeah." He muttered a few words in French.

Ashley smiled and said a small phrase in her own high school French, a little jealous of the European ease with languages. She hadn't thought the British spoke as many languages as continental Europeans, but she'd heard him use French before. "Where'd you learn French?"

"Summers abroad. You?"

"Mrs. Hart's third period French class. I finished French Two, but I'm nowhere as proficient as you. Teach me some?"

Caz bargained, "Maybe you could cook dinner for me again?"

"Okay." Ashley pressed the power button. "This first one is cool. I think you should assess the movies, see which kiss is your favorite so you can duplicate it. Or maybe do a combination of the kisses on the discs." She felt a little chatty and was generous with her advice.

Caz sighed. "I know how to kiss."

"Well, that kiss with Petra was bad," she said honestly.

Caz shrugged. "My character wouldn't kiss her. I wouldn't kiss her. It has no authenticity on either level."

What an artsy thing to say. Ashley tried to imagine a guy at her high school saying something like that. It would never happen. They'd see Petra in the red lingerie and that would be enough. Then again, no matter what the reason, she was glad Caz wouldn't kiss Petra. His rejection of her made this task okay somehow.

She cued up the scene then hit play.

Onscreen, the actor lifted the actress against his body and looked deep into her eyes. She looked longingly at him and then he kissed her and spun around. Her legs flew out, buoyed by each rotation of the spin.

"What's romantic about that?"

Ashley hit pause. "You're kidding?"

"Looks dizzy. What else did you bring?"

Ashley set her glass down and rose to switch out the first DVD for the second one.

Onscreen, the couple stood in the rain silently staring at each other. Then the actress dropped her little dog and flew into the hero's arms. The actor lifted her by the hips and gave her a passionate kiss. The rain cocooned them in its embrace and the only sound was the fall of the drops.

Ashley raised her eyebrows.

Caz wrinkled his nose and took a sip of his drink, clearly not impressed. "Looks cold, and drippy. And what happened to the dog?" He snagged the remote and rewound the disc to replay the dog part.

Kneeling on the cushion, she grabbed his arms. "He can't resist her. They don't feel the rain. Their passion is so intense they defy the elements."

Caz shook his head. "She lost her dog."

Pouting a little, Ashley got up to switch out the DVD for number three. How could he not like her choices? These were great romantic scenes, the best. "If all British people found the rain cold and drippy, there wouldn't be so many of you. It's romantic."

"We have indoors."

In DVD three, the onscreen couple eased from the water toward the shore. The night was dark, lit only by stars. Italian opera played softly in the background. The actress ran her hands lightly up the hero's arms and to his face. Rising on tiptoe, she leaned her bikini-clad body against his.

His hands went to her hips and yanked her flush against him. Bending slightly, he shoved the actress back into the sand and followed her down, pressing inch by inch against her until he lay fully on top. The sandy beach took on an imprint of their bodies.

Music swelled. The actor clasped her hands and raised them above her head then pressed his mouth against hers. Moaning, she wound her leg around his. The scene darkened.

Caz tilted his head. He looked from Ashley to the screen and hit pause. "Maybe. What do you like about that one?"

"The atmosphere. The music. And the contrast. She's all gentle and he's all alpha-manly."

Caz rose. "Okay, let's try it." He took her arm and led Ashley to the back of his trailer—to his bedroom.

CHAPTER 12

Her eyes widened at the sight of his bed. They'd put a wall-to-wall king-size bed in his trailer.

Caz grabbed a remote and clicked away at the buttons. Country music filled the room. "Because you're from Texas," he drawled.

She laughed, and leaned against the wall while he dimmed the lights. She hadn't known he could imitate her accent, and wanted to make him say more. The laughter eased her nerves, but the darkness was bringing it back—well, nerves and excitement. She'd been interested in kissing him again ever since his kiss in the hallway.

Caz dropped the remote and lifted an eyebrow in challenge. Ashley rubbed her arms then stepped close. *Okay, I can do this. This is fake. He's hot. It's only a kiss.* Lightly touching his hands and arms then his face, she felt sparks against her fingertips. Rising on her toes, she leaned toward his mouth. She floated her lips over his, then retreated.

His hands landed on her hips and pulled her forward, flat against him like in the video. She felt the roughness of his jeans and the hardness of his chest against her softness. His mouth landed on hers, warm, determined. She moved against him and closed off her mind to everything else. The sensations felt great. Caz lifted her and tossed her back.

Bouncing down to the mattress jolted Ashley out of the moment. Her arms flew out against the sheets, and she shook her head. "The throw looks better than it feels. I was getting into the kiss, and you broke the momentum."

Caz grinned at her complaint and leaned down carefully against her, most of his weight on his elbows.

Her eyelids lowered. "Mmm, okay, yeah, that's good."

Following the script, he grabbed her hands and raised them above her head. The new position took his weight from his elbows and put the bulk on her. For a second his body felt great, enticing, satisfying; then he was too heavy. Pulling her hands free, she shoved at his shoulders and he rolled to his back, his arm banging against the wall. Country music twanged in the background.

She crawled on top of him. "You're too big, you'll crush the poor girl. That actor must be one of those little short ones who looks large on screen." Grabbing his hands, she pulled them above his head and grinned at him. "How's that?"

Shaking his hands free, he slid his palms against her waist and under the hem of her shirt and used his fingers to brush against her skin. It made her squirm and her breathing shallow. She lowered against him.

"Hmm," Caz said. "You have to sacrifice for your art." He spoke in his own accent.

Her eyelids lowered and she wanted to crush his perfectly shaped lips against hers before his words fully registered. She lifted up. Caz said *art*. He was just practicing a scene. Ashley sucked in a breath. She shouldn't forget that; she was getting too involved with the kissing, as if the emotions were sincere. No wonder costars fell for each other—rehearsal kisses felt real. Backing away, she gave him a small pat on the knee. "Come on, three down, two to go." She slid off the bed.

Her legs weren't quite steady as she went back to the living room. She adjusted the hem of her shirt and leaned over to put in DVD number four. When she was certain he'd joined her, she hit the play button. The fourth scene came on.

The setting was a spaceship. The male actor was in a captain's chair. The actress straddled him and his hands rested against her hips. Her hands ran through his long hair and she kissed his neck above his pointy collar. He kept still. She used her teeth and tongue, striving for a reaction.

Suddenly, he moved. He kissed the skin of her shoulder over the strap of her sequined camisole then nipped at her collarbone. The actress shuddered against him and yanked his head back to press her lips hard against his. Rising on her knees, she straightened in order to lift his polyester tunic over his head. She tossed his uniform to the floor. "Oh, Dirk," the onscreen actress pleaded, "only you can help me save the planet." Rubbing his chest, she said, "Come with me to Quataria and free our fellow humans."

Dirk's mouth lifted from probing her ear and an orange-striped lizard tongue slid free, flicking into the air. He said, "I am a Quatarian."

The actress screamed.

Caz looked at Ashley with raised eyebrows. She grinned and grabbed disc five. “Okay, that one was a mistake. Or, I should have stopped the clip before he finished probing her ear.”

Caz stilled her hand. “No, I’d do that one.” Taking disc five from her, he set it on the couch then lifted Ashley onto his lap. She smiled at him and straddled his legs. She’d kind of wanted to do this one too. He had a nice neck and he always smelled like soap, shampoo, and Caz. Leaning forward, she kissed his skin then tasted him with her tongue. His skin was smooth. He must have shaved before she came over. He tasted salty and clean, unique. Using her other hand, she brushed against the other side of his neck and continued.

His hand tugged down the neck of her shirt to expose her shoulder. Caz ran his tongue from her shoulder to her collarbone. The sensation made her bite down lightly against his neck. He returned the gesture on her collarbone, causing an electric feeling.

In reaction, she sucked his skin between her teeth then released him. Her forehead fell forward against his shoulder, and she trembled. Feeling adrift, she clenched her hands against his sides. Using his hands to lean her back a little, he nibbled.

She reached for him. Lifting his wrist to her mouth, she ran her tongue over the inside and gave it a kiss. A faint tremor went through his powerful body and then he stilled. Her gaze fell on his mouth; her memory made her want to feel it. Ashley swallowed and tried to suck in a breath.

Caz lifted his head, his eyes on hers. Ashley dropped his wrist and her fingers landed against DVD five. She lifted the disc and shoved it against his chest, trying to calm her heart rate.

His hand landed over the top of hers. He took his own deep breath. Their hands rose and she wanted to slide her hand under his shirt. She pulled free and reached down for his hem.

Looking at DVD number five, Caz rose, sliding her off his lap. She fell back against the couch cushion and watched him. He inserted the DVD into the player and the images appeared. DVD five displayed another scene in the rain.

The actor stood close to the actress and he rubbed his hands against her sides. She moaned and leaned into him. His hands slid over her breasts and cupped the back of her neck, and he kissed her.

Ashley’s eyes widened. She’d forgotten how risqué this one was, how hot.

The damp of the weather made their clothes see-through. One of his hands slid under her thigh. He lifted her leg against him, then ran his other hand down to her other thigh to lift it too. She grabbed his shoulders to hold on while he supported her weight with his hands beneath her butt. The actress squirmed against the hero.

Caz hit stop before the scene even finished. "We can do that."

"Uh. The weather's rainy too. You already vetoed the water scenes."

Caz held out a hand, and Ashley took it, unable to resist following him down the hallway. After opening a narrow door in the hall, he pushed her inside. His bathroom smelled like his shower gel. She took a deep breath and looked at him curiously. He stuck a hand into the stall and turned the water on.

Ashley laughed, relaxing, and resisted when he pushed her toward the water. "These are my only clothes."

Caz lifted off his shirt and her laughter stopped. He had such a nice chest. How would his skin look covered in raindrops? She lifted a hand in his direction and her fingers trembled when she reached the skin of his abdomen. Flattening her palm against him, she stepped forward and raised her gaze to his mouth. She needed to feel his lips on hers. The nerves in her hand tingled as she rubbed against his skin.

He reached for the hem of her shirt and she let him lift it, helping him pull the material free from her head and arms. It dropped to the floor. She slid her left arm around his neck and her right around the warm skin at his waist. Arching, she leaned against his hardness, pressing into him—the feel of skin on skin amazing, wonderful. Ashley lifted her mouth toward his. "Mmm."

His hands ran from her shoulders to her waist, sending sensations shooting throughout her body to her toes. Her knee raised and she hooked it around his leg to draw him closer. His head tilted and his mouth met hers with a moan. The kiss was magic, open and deep. All control lost.

Tap, tap, tap.

From the other side of the shower door, she heard a male voice, the AD.

"Caz, you in there?"

Ashley blinked. The interruption pulled her from the glow of sensation too fast, from bliss to bewildered in one second flat. Trying to convince her body to cooperate, she stepped back, shaking. Caz resisted for a moment. Then he let her go and muttered a curse. Ashley bent down to grab her shirt from the floor and pulled it on.

Tap, tap, tap. "Caz? Can you hear me?" the AD asked louder.

Glowering at the door, Caz stepped backward and shut the water off. "I should have locked the trailer," he said quietly to her.

"We've got some new script pages for you that'll fix that scene with Petra," the AD said. His voice was louder and clearer without the water running.

Caz reached around her to open his bathroom door.

The AD glanced between them curiously and said, "Hi," like he found them together in bathroom stalls every day. Next, he handed Caz some pages. "Here are the new sheets. You'll lead the vixen to the bedroom and strip off your shirt. Then when she thinks she has you where she wants you, you'll stop."

Ashley stepped around Caz and into the hallway. Her mouth felt swollen. Her face felt hot.

"It's a real power move. Your character fully realizing that the vixen is a part of the conspiracy. It's great." The AD looked carefully at Ashley. "You'd better leave so he can learn the new lines."

"Okay." Ashley went to the living room to gather the DVDs.

The AD followed her and settled into a spot on the couch. He lifted a page of the script and stared at Caz expectantly.

Caz frowned as she left, but he didn't stop her.

***

Ashley tugged the emerald green sheet over the corner of the mattress and one of the other corners popped off. She'd short-sheeted the bed. A sigh huffed out of her mouth. She flipped the sheet around and redid all the corners. Last night, she'd kissed Caz, really kissed him, and today she had to put sheets on the bed where he'd roll around with another woman. Hollywood. Once the director had found out that Lorene would be here today, he'd rearranged the whole schedule to accommodate her. Today they'd shoot the second love scene, the one with Caz's character and his true love Aurora.

Which kiss would Caz choose? Ashley knew she had no right to feel put out, but she hated the thought of watching him with someone else. That would be her punishment for getting carried away last night. He was an actor, not her boyfriend; what had she been thinking? Ashley threw the flat sheet over the top and grabbed the fluffy comforter.

"Hurry up." Cutter paced near the entrance to the costume area. "I need your help with the wedding gown." He paced some more, muttering while she spread the satin comforter over the sheets. "The gown is priceless. I can't believe we're changing the schedule. I need to fit her."

All the costumes were prepared in advance of filming, but Cutter performed adjustments and repairs on set. He wrung his hands. "This gown will be in a ton of flashback sequences. Every line has to fit perfectly."

Boomer and a stagehand wheeled a squeaky mobile clothing rack past them into the dressing area.

Cutter said, "Be careful with those," and scurried over to right a blue dress that was inches from falling off its hanger.

"PA," the AD called.

Ashley released the pillow she'd cased and headed his way. The AD was talking to Cutter at the rack, and whatever he said made Cutter stiffen and charge into the main characters' dressing room.

Ashley followed them into the dressing room, which was filled with mobile closets, labeled clothes, privacy screens, and long mirrors. "What's going on?"

Before the AD could answer, Cutter scooped up a measuring tape and a pair of scissors, a panicked expression on his face. "PA."

"What do you need?" Olive wore new running shoes and she'd attached some black binder clips to a string around her waist.

"I need—"

The AD held up his hand to Cutter. "Wait. PA, I need you to run these pages up to the executives' office."

"I'll do it," Ashley said, thinking she could say *hi* to her dad.

Olive snagged the papers from the AD's hand. "You're assigned to Cutter today."

Ashley reached over to take the papers from Olive, but she backed away fast and trotted toward the door. Short of chasing her, the errand belonged to Olive. Ashley eyed her short legs and small feet. She could catch her.

The AD chuckled and Ashley swung back to him, but her gaze was caught by an actress stumbling from behind a privacy screen. She had perfect skin, red hair long enough to swing around her waist, and wore a short lime silk robe. Lorene.

Lorene's amber eyes stabbed a hole in Cutter, and she slurred her words. "I'm not an eight, I'm a six." The actress stepped forward and almost fell. She stayed upright by grabbing the side of the dressing screen and using it to steady her legs.

"You were a four when we fit the dress," Cutter said to her. He used his hands to demonstrate the differences in those two sizes, stretching out as far as he could reach. From the green hue covering her perfect skin, Lorene didn't appreciate his exaggeration.

The AD said, "Lorene's here. Place her in the hoop so we can get the blocking done. Recut the dress later."

Cutter gasped as if the director had proposed mass murder. "It's a Harlon Ramonannini wedding dress. The silk cannot be recut. It can only be revered."

The AD suggested, "Add elastic."

Cutter paled and let out a whimper.

Adding to the sounds of misery in the room, Lorene groaned and wiped a hand over her sweaty forehead. “Where’s the makeup lady? I need makeup.” She followed that request with a retching belch.

Ashley backed up a step, and someone brushed by her from behind. Petra.

Petra swaggered into the dressing area without a word of greeting and went straight to a mobile closet rack. She flipped through the costumes. After finding what she was looking for, she waved a red outfit at Cutter. “You don’t mind, do you?” Without waiting for his response, she stripped off her shirt. “I’ll need to switch out my jewelry too.”

Ashley quickly looked away because she knew that Petra would keep stripping. Her nudity had lost its shock value because Petra walked around without clothes no matter who was there. Even so, Ashley had no interest in seeing more. She wished there was a way to un-see what she’d already seen. Her gaze returned to Lorene.

Evidently, Lorene and Petra knew each other. The redhead weaved toward the disrobing brunette and latched a hand onto Petra’s mobile closet. Her weight jolted the rack and the hangers swung outward, threatening to dump the clothes. A few of the empty hangers clattered to the floor. The crew working in the room paused and turned at the sound.

Petra slid off her gray skirt with supreme indifference and slipped on a new cranberry-colored one. “I’ll need rubies or garnets.”

“If I’d a known you’d be on set today,” Lorene said, “I’d have had a drink.”

“Yeah, that’s what you need, another drink.” Petra turned to Cutter. “I’m borrowing a costume.” She tucked her blouse in and smoothed her hands over her hips. “*I* have an interview with the press. *I* show up for work.”

“What a shock,” Lorene said. “There’s a camera and there you are.”

“She actually helps the movie by doing press,” Cutter said in Petra’s defense. He picked up a fallen hanger and returned it to the rack.

Lorene snorted.

“God,” Petra said, staring the actress up and down. “Cutter’s right. How large are you? I’d help with the blocking, but I’m only a size zero. I’m always a size zero or a double zero. You can ask anyone. They all know I’m a size zero.”

“Zero brain. And the leading men always go for me, and you go home alone.” Lorene stepped closer to Petra. The wheels on the mobile closet slid sideways. Cutter jumped clear, keeping an anxious eye on the swinging costumes.

Olive was going to be so pissed she missed the drama, Ashley thought, and wondered how the AD would break up the argument.

Petra wiggled to adjust the fit on the skirt. "Leading men maybe, but the leading part? Those always go to me."

Lorene gurgled.

"I don't have any scenes with you, thank God." Petra eyed Lorene's frame. "I'm smaller framed than you, but I could carry off more weight. I could go up several sizes. More than you, and the weight would work on me because of how I'm built." She sniffed and turned to Cutter. "This is perfect. The color is so me. Cranberry is the new garnet. I'm going to—"

"I'm the—" Lorene bent toward Petra and heaved the contents of her stomach.

Ew. Ashley pulled the neck of her T-shirt over her nose so she wouldn't have to smell the spew.

Lorene fell to her knees and retched. Cutter threw himself in front of the clothes to protect them. Petra began a piercing shriek, which made Lorene clutch at her head and glare upwards. "Shut up," Lorene said between gags.

"Lush," Petra said.

Ashley, suddenly worried she'd have to perform some type of nursing or janitorial duty, took quick steps back and out of the dressing room. She kept her nose covered until she cleared the area.

It didn't seem as if she'd like Lorene any more than she liked Petra. How unfortunate. Poor Lorene, though; Ashley hated getting sick. Powder would have to double up on her makeup to conceal the green in her complexion. Ashley smiled a little and was no longer jealous at the thought of Caz's kissing soul mate scene—good luck to him. She curled up on a counter in the makeup station and took out her notebook, intending to sketch until the drama died down. Using the edge of her pencil, she added shading and hadn't done more than half the page before she heard them again.

"It's worse than that." Cutter's voice rose dramatically with each word. "She's a balloon. She was already a jumbo-sized four." He came into view and Ashley watched as he held out his arms around his body in a balloon shape and wobbled from one leg to the other like a two-week-overdue pregnant lady. "Now she's a gargantuan size eight." Cutter tipped sideways as if he'd fall to the ground, kicking one foot out, shaking it like a dog.

"Stop it," Ashley said. "Eight's not big."

"Fine," Cutter said. "Then you squeeze my size four Harlon Ramonannini wedding dress on her. Oh wait. You can't. Lorene's in the toilet, vomiting." He wrinkled his nose and ran his eyes from the top of her head to her tennis shoes. "No wonder you're defending her, you're another jumbo. What size are you?"

"Shut up."

The AD said, "No, answer him. What size are you?"

Ashley glared at him too. Hollywood. "Three."

The AD shoved his hand through his hair. "Thank God. Problem solved. Put the hoop skirt on the PA, and she can do the blocking. We'll work with Lorene when she sobers up." The AD looked around the makeup area and called, "Powder."

Ashley tucked her notebook into her bag and whipped out her cell phone. She shot off a text to Marissa. "Preparing to wear a hoop skirt. Dignity in jeopardy. How is Fry Hut?"

Marissa's reply was immediate. "Dignity long lost. Restoration hopes limited."

"Hurry up," Cutter said. "You're ruining the schedule."

Powder showed up and raised a pierced eyebrow. She wore a green micro mini, a purple sweater, and messy hair.

The AD said, "Lorene's sick. Put Ashley in her makeup until we can get Lorene ready."

Ashley put her phone back in her bag and moved closer to Powder. "Like the purple highlights."

"Thanks." Powder tossed her some face cream. Ashley slathered the lotion on her face and neck while Powder loaded a tray marked *Lorene* onto a wheeled cart. "Glad the reporter wasn't here today. That's a real trinity of stars, ego, drunk, and Caz."

"Hair," the AD called. Another lady, one Ashley didn't know very well, went to work pulling her hair back tight while Powder prepped her face. Powder kept up a running chatter about her date last night.

"Did he wear a button-down shirt?"

"Sweater vest, it was just as bad," Powder said. "But man, was he hot when the argyles hit the floor."

Cutter stood in the makeup area the whole time, pacing and muttering.

The makeup artist and hair stylist were pros, so they ignored him. A few pokes, pulls, and jabs later, and Ashley was transformed into Aurora—Lorene's character.

"Thanks."

"Break a leg," Powder said.

Ashley joined Cutter. "I'm ready."

Cutter wasn't his usual pristine self, with mussed hair and an untucked shirt. "This is a disaster. A catastrophe. Are you really a three? Because you don't look like a three. I can squeeze you in, if you're close."

"Yes. It'll be fine." Ashley followed Cutter over to the dressing area. She went slowly, hesitant to see what disaster was left behind.

Instead, there was only beauty. Caz stood with a few of the other male actors dressing in tuxedos. She didn't know if he looked good because he could kiss or if he just looked good in a tuxedo, but the scene was a way better view than earlier. She hesitated in the doorway.

Cutter prodded her forward. "Quit getting distracted. We're late."

Ashley nodded; Cutter was right. The guys had a later call time than the girls because their hair, makeup, and costumes went quicker. If the guys were already dressing, then the girls should be done.

Cutter drew her to a mobile closet away from the guys, but she responded to Caz's wave of greeting. Caz started toward her but was pulled back by an assistant threading a tie under his collar. The guys were abuzz with gossip about this morning and Caz looked bored with the discussion. Evidently, vomiting drunks weren't headline news to the British.

Cutter tugged on the waist of Ashley's T-shirt, pulling her attention away from the men in tuxedos.

Just because Petra and some of the others stripped off in public didn't mean she would. Ashley slapped his hand away and pointed at the privacy screens along the back wall. She wanted a privacy screen and a lock if they had one.

"Fine." Cutter let go of the cotton. He snagged a labeled dressing bag off the rack and flounced his way over to one of the screens. He held the dressing bag out with a stiff arm. "Yell when you're ready."

Ashley stepped carefully across the floor, relieved to see no physical evidence of this morning's mishap. She took hold of the hanger.

Cutter unzipped the bag and withdrew a muslin-covered hoop and a white satin corset. "Put on the framework and I'll help you guide the wedding gown over them."

Ashley took the garments from him and went behind the screen. Though her view was gone, she could still hear everyone in the vicinity. Dressing while people stood a few feet away talking was weird. She hesitated with her hands on the button of her jeans.

Act like it's the mall dressing room. She let go and stepped into the hoop then kicked her jeans off. She tied the bow at her waist and rolled her hips to watch the hoop sway. When the edge knocked into the screen, she stopped.

One more piece. Ashley pulled the corset on backwards so she could latch most of it then drug her T-shirt off. She inched the corset into proper position and pulled the cups up over her bra. She couldn't reach the back so she left the top hooks unfastened. Nor could she do anything about her purple bra straps. Well, maybe she could tuck them into the dress. She'd see what Cutter suggested.

After emerging from behind the screen, Cutter took her arm and drew her in front of a three-way mirror. "Okay, okay, that fits," Cutter said in relief. His hands went to the hooks between her shoulder blades, and he did them up while muttering, "Suck it in." He made a noise of satisfaction when the last one closed. "PA."

Ashley turned, but Cutter was talking to Olive. He and Olive lifted the white silk wedding dress carefully up and over. A full thirty seconds passed in darkness as the complicated silk gown was draped over her head. When the fabric cleared and she could see again, her eyes met Olive's hostile gaze.

Olive said, "I've been reassigned to costumes all day." Her leaden hazel glare put the blame on Ashley's shoulders.

While Cutter twittered around Ashley, adjusting pieces of white silk, Olive did up the numerous small pearl buttons that ran the back of the dress.

"What kind of model wears purple underwear?" Olive snapped the elastic of Ashley's bra strap.

"Ouch. Don't."

In a quick motion, Cutter pulled the straps down her arms to her elbows. Ashley threw her hands over the front of her chest.

Cutter said, "The corset serves as a bra."

Ashley felt her bra loosen and pull free. She kept her palms tight on the bodice while Cutter yanked her bra away. This was the first time a guy had removed her bra, and the moment was not at all like she'd imagined. At a minimum, she'd hoped he'd be straight.

Cutter tossed the purple lace to Olive.

The AD came back in the room. "Does the dress fit?"

Cutter said, "Yes," with deep satisfaction and fussed with the hem.

The AD ran a critical eye over Ashley and nodded.

Caz walked over and stood beside him. He stared at Ashley a moment, then at the purple bra lying across the chair back, where Olive had tossed it.

Cutter tugged Ashley's arms down and adjusted the silk bodice. "She overflows the top a bit, but not too much." He released the bodice and reached a hand up to shove at her chest. "Why'd you order such large boobs? The trend is flat. These don't work with the flounce."

Ashley slapped his hand away. "They're real."

Olive snorted. "Sure they are."

"Who knew she had them under those T-shirts?" Cutter paced back and forth, assessing the flounce. Any other guy she'd accuse of checking out her cleavage. His eyes were solidly on the flounce.

Caz moved behind her, and she checked his reflection in the mirror. His gaze was not on the flounce. Ashley crossed her arms over her chest.

Caz raised his eyes and met hers. “I told my agent to try working in a holiday after the film.”

“Good.”

The AD took Caz’s arm, urging him away. “We’ll see you on set.”

Cutter paced two steps and made a type of moan. Then he turned on his heel and went to a kit. After that, he didn’t hesitate. He snipped at the ruffle covering her cleavage, and the thin chiffon detached from the top. He picked at a few threads, ignoring her slapping hands. When he was done, he turned her back to face the mirror.

“Beautiful,” Cutter said, “My dress is beautiful.”

CHAPTER 13

Wearing the wig and wedding gown, Ashley didn't recognize herself. The gown cascaded in complicated silk drapes, and removing the flounce improved the beautiful dress to a ridiculous degree. She wanted to spend more time staring at her image through her fake eyelashes, but the extras were in place and they wanted to run through the scene. That involved checking the lighting and making small changes to the sets and costumes. Then they'd shoot as much as they could and film close-ups with Lorene this afternoon, or if Lorene couldn't be sobered up enough for that today, they'd shoot the close-ups tomorrow.

That schedule gave Cutter a short deadline to find a size eight wedding dress comparable to the elaborate one worn by Ashley, so the AD sent Olive to help Cutter search.

This bridal gown was gorgeous. Ashley would have to remember to ask Powder to snap a picture of her wearing it with all the makeup and wig. The photo would make a great memento of her job, and Mom would love it. She swayed in the hoop, wondering if Marissa's fry costume had a similar type of framework or if it was all foam padding. After her last hip sway threatened to take out a lamp, she stepped more carefully onto the stage.

This time, she wasn't nervous. She'd helped map out blocking a number of times, plus there was no way they'd make her hold the tape and mark the floor in this dress. Standing around would be easy.

The main director was shooting today. He'd looked her over with a nod and started calling her "Aurora," the name of the long-lost love. Being called *Aurora* was a distinct step up from being called *PA*.

"Walk down the aisle toward Caz, clasp his hands, and stare into his eyes." The director turned to the sound guy. "I want music. Fold the song for the scene and I'll let you know where to mark it."

The haunting ballad "Love's Romantic Ruin" came on and Ashley wedding-marched down the aisle, past about fifty extras, wearing a tentative smile for Caz. They were only shooting her from the back. The camera's focus would be on the groom and Lorene's image would be cut in later. She was near enough to see his face, his hopeful and loving expression. The look really wasn't anything like the real Caz, so she grinned. Her smile widened and her steps became more certain. When she reached him, she took his warm hand and let him draw her close. A fake maid of honor took the prop bouquet of pink silk flowers from her, leaving Ashley to stare at Caz for the next few minutes—not a bad way to earn a living. She whispered, "If you shoot out an orange lizard tongue at me, I'll scream."

His grin deepened, and for a second it was the real Caz's smile. The director made her repeat the march down the aisle several times and with each take, they played the same song in the background. Ashley knew she'd hear "Love's Romantic Ruin" in her head for the rest of the day.

The location moved to a bedroom. The AD noted that usually the bride changed into a going-away dress for the honeymoon suite, not her wedding gown.

Cutter had returned and he had a fit over that suggestion. "We're featuring that dress. You wanted romantic, and that dress epitomizes romance. The white silk has visual impact, the cascade drama."

"I agree," the director said. "Leave it on, Aurora."

The AD protested, "But we want to keep as much of this shot as we can, and Cutter's having problems with the replacement dress. It doesn't match. That gown is a one of a kind."

"We're shooting dark and candlelit, and we can tweak the images with the computers if we have to, blurring it."

Cutter moaned. "I'll search harder."

The AD nodded. He made a rolling motion and the song kicked on again. The crew adjusted prop candles around the king-size bed. Ashley looked at the green sheets and folded her arms over her waist. She wasn't nervous to kiss Caz. He tasted great, but she didn't want to be judged on how she looked kissing, not that they could see much of her under the wig. She caught her reflection in the mirror and the foreignness helped calm her pulse. Long curly red wig, wedding gown—she didn't look like herself at all.

"No, no," the director said. "Ashley, isn't it?"

Ashley looked toward him in surprise. Again, she had a name. She nodded.

"Keep that virginal-terror look you had a second ago." The director moved behind a camera. "The expression worked."

Crap, they were judging her already and they hadn't even gotten to the kiss yet. She bit her lip. She wasn't an actress. Which kiss did Caz want to do? He needed to tell her. She tried to catch his eyes and ask, but he didn't meet her gaze. His eyes were on her mouth.

Next, she heard some information about the take, "Sound speed. Roll camera. Speed."

Powder appeared in front of her and slicked strawberry-vanilla-flavored gloss across her lips, then spritzed breath spray in her mouth. Ashley coughed as the wintergreen hit her tongue. The clapper guy called out, "Marker" and clicked the clapperboard shut.

She looked at Caz and didn't have to fake the virginal terror. They were definitely taping this. This situation was doubly critical because Caz had blown the other kiss. The directors were all watching, geared to criticize. The situation was different when the eyes were on you, and she wished she'd been a little more sensitive in offering her opinion back in the viewing room.

Music swelled and lights dimmed. That helped. Caz took her hand and led her to the bed, while shrugging out of his tuxedo jacket, kicking off his shoes, and pulling at his tie. His expression was intent and loving, not one of Caz's usual expressions. Once they were beside the bed, he gave her a gentle kiss then pushed at her arms until she sat.

The gown puffed around her. From the bed, Ashley looked up at Caz with a smile. This was a better way of hitting the mattress than the throw they'd practiced in the trailer. He was learning fast, thanks to his teacher.

Caz lifted a cufflinked wrist to her and raised his eyebrows. Ashley grinned again. He'd liked that wrist kiss thing. Slipping the metal stud from the French cuff, she leaned across him to place the link on the bedside table. His expression showed gentle passion. She lifted his wrist, shoved the cuff up, and bent her head to glide her lips over his skin.

Grasping her arms to raise her to her feet, he pulled her closer, but the hoop prevented him from reeling her in. Ashley smiled and shoved at the sea of fabric. This scene was going to need several takes. Caz leaned over sideways and removed her high heels. She balanced with hands against his shoulders.

After flinging the white satin pumps across the room, Caz turned her so that her back was to him. Gently pushing her hair over her shoulder, he undid the first pearl button. With each two undone, he placed a kiss on her back. She shivered. Midway through, she turned in his arms and grasped his shirt. She pulled the ends loose from his trousers.

His hands went to her back and he began blindly working on the rest of the gown's buttons. Ashley undid the buttons of his dress shirt and pulled the sides open. The more film they could get of Caz with his shirt off, the better. Caz shrugged free and stepped back to pull his undershirt over his head. She paused a moment to admire the view. *Wow.* His workout routine paid off. Her hands went to his shoulders and she lightly kissed the side of his neck.

His hands were busy at the back of her dress. When the buttons were undone to her waist, he untied the hoop's bow. Once loosened, the stringed closure fell open and the hoop dropped to the floor beneath the wedding dress. Caz groaned at his success and he pulled her flush against him. Backing up to the bed, he sat and pulled her close. She straddled his legs, her knees against the mattress. Shoving at the yards of silk, she smiled, knowing the kiss he'd chosen.

Caz tugged at the top of the dress and she let it slide down her arms, leaving her wearing the corset, which was much more than Petra usually wore around the set. He kissed her neck, her shoulder, and her collarbone. Ashley shoved him against the bed so she could lie against him.

He put one arm around her hips and one hand behind her head and kissed her while rolling her over so that he was on top. He felt great, not too heavy at all. Their mouths clung and their legs tangled. Digging her fingers into his shoulders, she pulled him closer and ran a hand down his back. Her leg lifted over his hips, and she shifted to pull him tighter. She felt him push at the hem of her gown, sliding the silk up her calf until his hand rested against her knee. She moaned against his mouth. His hand slid around to the underside of her knee and his fingers played against her skin. She gasped against his lips, and no longer heard the song in her head, the sparks drowned out the lyrics.

"Okay," the director said. "That's good."

Ashley slid her fingers into Caz's hair. His teeth touched her bottom lip, demanding wider. She ran a tongue against their edge and opened.

"Perfect, I think you got it guys." The director laughed.

The laughter shook her out of the moment. Ashley pulled back in confusion, resisting Caz's searching mouth, and looked over his shoulder.

His mouth went to her neck.

Her eyelids closed.

"Cut."

***

Today, Aurora died. Ashley, wearing the character's wig and sundress, had to walk over to a car, wave at Caz with a smile, then reach for the door handle. After that, the director would add in the green screen stunt with Aurora flying backwards to her demise.

They scheduled the explosion scene first because they needed the daylight to shoot it. Lorene would arrive this afternoon to record wedding vows, the honeymoon scene, and the wave. The actor's day would be tremendously long, but they weren't relenting. Keeping on schedule meant everything on a film's budget. The studio had decided not to replace Lorene after a pleading call from her agent and because her scenes were really short.

"Ashley," the director called.

She turned, still startled at not being called *PA*.

"We had some hiccups in the scene where you take Caz his tea. Do you mind taking this cup over to Caz?" The director handed her a cup of coffee and nodded toward the stage.

"Sure, but you know he doesn't drink coffee."

"It's for the character."

Ashley joined him. "Here." She set the cup down on the prop desk. Caz wore the uniform of a rookie police officer.

Caz sniffed at the cup, smelling the coffee. "That's not tea."

Ashley rolled her eyes. "I know, the director said to give it to you."

"You know I drink tea."

"I know. If you say that one more time, I'm not going to be happy."

"I know." Caz grinned at her and pulled her onto his lap.

She threw her arms around his shoulders to steady herself, half-laughing.

Caz said, "Will you share with me later?"

"Maybe."

"Caz," the director said. "Lift her onto the desk and give her a kiss. Garrett, walk in and make a remark."

Ashley blinked in surprise, but Caz moved before she could question the plan. He lifted her onto the desk and stepped between her jean-clad legs. "Want to go house hunting with me later?"

"Don't you have a Realtor?"

"Diane. I've been with her. She's getting impatient with me."

"Do I get a vote on which you pick?"

"Maybe." Caz kissed her. His lips felt firm and warm. She wound a hand into his hair and straightened to get closer. Her other arm slid to his waist.

Garrett's character said, "On your own time."

Caz pulled back and helped Ashley off the desk.

***

"What do you think about this one?" Diane, the Realtor, waved a hand toward the view below. The house was a sleek, modern, glass-walled home that clung to the side of a hill. The structure reminded her of Diane, with her slim-fit modern suit, clinging to her cell phone.

Ashley wasn't a fan of heights so she stayed far away from the open glass window. "Can paparazzi shoot through the glass? Or is his privacy protected in some way?"

"I'm sure it's fine," Diane said. "If privacy's one of Caspian's concerns he can get curtains."

Caz looked uncomfortable and didn't seem to like this house at all. Nor had he liked the last house. That one had been rustic in style and had also clung to the side of a hill.

"Why don't we look at some places in the city, near the studio?" Diane said. "We can save the beach properties for last."

Caz nodded and Ashley followed them back out to Diane's silver Lexus. Diane kept up a monologue the whole way, not giving Caz or Ashley time to answer. "Though the Hollywood Hills is really where it's at. You can't get anything like this view. And the resale. Well, I assume you'll be going back to England? So resale's certainly an important factor."

The expression in Caz's eyes was wild with a touch of hunted antelope. Diane was asking him his life plan. He was an actor. Ashley would bet he couldn't say what he wanted for dinner, much less where he'd want to retire. Diane let it drop and they checked out city lofts next.

The first loft they looked at reminded her of Petra's place but smaller. The loft had been convenient to the studio, but modern and soul-less. "Now, if you're planning to start a family soon," Diane said, "this won't work at all, though people do raise families here. It's not unheard of."

For heaven's sake, he was only a year older than Ashley; how old did Diane think they were? She bit her lip and pulled out her digital camera as Caz's wild-eyed look got wilder. "Point out any small thing you like or dislike so I can get a shot of it." Caz thrummed a hand on the granite kitchen counter, but didn't offer an opinion. She sighed. He would have to be led gently. Turning to Diane, she said, "May we wander around for a bit?"

"Of course," Diane said, and hovered in the background.

Ashley wondered how Caz had gotten stuck with such an annoying Realtor.

Diane pointed at the skylights. "Note the natural light. This is a very green choice for you."

Caz looked up dutifully. Ashley held up her camera, took a shot, then pointed it at the countertop. “Caz, do you like this color?” With one hand, she patted the top.

“Yes.”

Ashley snapped a photo.

“That’s not the worst reason to buy a property,” Diane said. “Love is love. You should snap this place up.”

Ashley had searched house-hunting tips online after she’d agreed to go. “I read that you should mainly look at the structure. The things you can’t change.” Ashley went back into the master bedroom and through to the master bath. The rooms in this loft smelled stale. The space must’ve been vacant for a while. “Do you like the separate his and her sinks or do you want a totally separate bathroom from your woman?”

Caz shrugged. “It rather depends on the girl, right?”

Ashley snapped a photo.

“Well, separate, of course, is the new trend,” Diane said. “But this is an older property, so you have some location advantages and give up some of the modern trends. You can always renovate.”

“Powder would probably turn one of the guest bedrooms into a dressing area.”

“Is Powder your partner?” Diane said. “Your daughter? Should we book when she can be here? How many kids are you planning on? Just a ballpark number will help.”

Ashley sighed again as Diane pushed on. It was like she was doing her best to blow the sale. Was this her first time out with a single guy?

Diane moved closer. “How about a place with separate quarters? You know, in case you have a buddy/entourage who want to live close?”

Ashley had to shut her down or they’d never get a word out of Caz. “I work for the studio, so I am sure you respect that we need to control the flow of information. There are some things he can’t answer right now. I’m sure you understand, having worked with famous people before.”

“I’m really only at the gathering information stage.” Caz said.

“Of course, but we all need a little push now and again or we wouldn’t get anywhere now, would we?” Diane gave a big wink. “Are there any British-type concerns you might have about a property in the States?”

“You mean like taxes?”

“Oh no, no, your real estate attorney and the title company will work all that out. I meant like foreign features.”

“Oh,” Ashley said. “That’s kind of interesting. You mean like Tudor-style? Eaves? A dormer?”

“Well, of course, certainly those things can matter, but I meant what you live with,” Diane said. “We can bring in some of those touches from home: beer on tap, and separate faucets for hot and cold water. One client even installed one of those red phone booths."

Caz shrugged.

"Clearly, you need to do more thinking. We won't run out to any of the out-of-town ranches today. But I do want to go down to the shore and get your reaction."

Ashley wondered how hard it would be to get a different Realtor.

CHAPTER 14

The beach house had a crazy layout. The guest room overlooked the water instead of the master and the balcony hung off the kitchen. Ashley slid the glass door open and stepped outside. Caz stood at the rail staring at the crashing waves. He turned to her with bright eyes. "I'd like a holiday by the water."

Diane joined them and jumped all over the gleam. "There are lots of interested parties for this house. You'll have to act fast with a strong bid to win this one. We can put down earnest money right away and close by early next month."

Ashley wasn't sure what earnest money was, but she was sure Caz wasn't ready for this decision. She shook her head. "He's only begun to look."

"This isn't it," Caz said.

"Now, don't be too hasty. You need to think about what you want, not what your girlfriend wants."

"It isn't what I want," Ashley said. "The layout of this house is ridiculous."

"It has character and charm."

Ashley bit out firmly, "He doesn't want it."

Caz shot her a sideways look and quirked up a corner of his mouth. He was the first to turn back to the car, his arm slung over her shoulders.

Traveling north on 110, Ashley sketched highlights of what she'd seen in her notebook while Caz and Diane argued.

"I'll know it when I see it," Caz said.

"That's not tremendously helpful."

"It is to me," Caz said. "Isn't it, Ashley?"

"Yes. Don't rush the decision." Caz was spending a fortune by anyone's standards. Diane pushing him wasn't helping.

"Fine," Diane said. "Call me when you at least pick an area of town and I'll find out what's available there. You can't sit on things out here. The California market is not like the market in England." They'd met Diane on set earlier that morning. It was now four o'clock. Skipping lunch had fueled everyone's annoyance.

Ashley poked Caz in the arm. ""Want to eat dinner at my place? We can go over the photos on my laptop. I have some design books here. You can flip through and see which styles you like."

He nodded. "I could rent, and you could draw blueprints for me."

Ashley smiled. "I couldn't draft you a tent. It'll be like seven years before I could design something for you."

"There is no advantage to building new," Diane said stiffly.

"Would you mind dropping us off in Fairville?" Ashley asked Diane.

"Sure." Diane looked somewhat pleased—probably because dad's house was fifteen minutes closer compared to the studio, meaning she could dump them out that much quicker. The car braked in front the mansion and Diane put the car in park, her gaze assessed the property while she pressured Caz. "I know all about your parents from the news. So this is definitely the time for you to buy your own place. Give them freedom with their shifting life plans."

Without responding, Caz shoved the door with one hand. He left the door open behind him and walked over to the pedestrian gate.

Diane glanced from Dad's house to Ashley and back. She spoke with her head tilted and her gaze glued to the mansion. "Anytime you want to go out again, let me know. Caz has my cell, and you both can reach me twenty-four, seven."

"Thanks."

"So nice to meet you, dear, I know you were a great help to Caspian today."

***

Caz followed her in and across the marble toward the kitchen. "Nice place."

"Thanks, it's my dad's." Ashley tossed her bag on the granite counter, breathing in the smell of Dad's kitchen—lemon cleaner and disuse. It smelled nothing like Mom's. "Mom and I live on a much more normal, suburban scale in north Houston."

His mouth twisted and something hard entered his eyes. "Do your parents still see each other, or no because your mum's in Texas?"

"Mom usually spends summers with me here. She's a teacher, so she has the time off."

"She always stays here? With you and your dad?"

"Yeah, they're friends."

Caz snorted, disbelief written over his face as if she'd said a politician had been faithful.

"No, really, they get along great. She's visiting only occasionally this summer because of my job, but she used to stay most of the summer. What? Your parents don't get along?"

"Dad comes around between girlfriends. He can't be alone and Mum takes him back every time, no matter what he's done." His voice sounded blasé, but his fists clenched for a moment and frustrated rage flickered through his eyes.

Ashley made a sympathetic humming noise, but didn't comment.

Caz looked around again, his shoulders relaxing. "Why are you working as an assistant if you live here? It can't pay that much."

"I'm an unpaid intern."

His eyebrows rose high on his forehead, meeting the edge of his lighter blond bangs, and he said, "You take a lot of crap for a volunteer."

"Don't I know it." Ashley opened the fridge and removed a covered dish holding two steaks marinating in one of Marissa's recipes. The steaks would've been grilled last night, but Dad hadn't been able to make dinner again, so Caz was in luck. She also scooped out the bowl of salad she'd put together: spinach, apples, cranberries, and bleu cheese crumbles. She carried the dishes through the French doors to the tiled patio. "Do you want a new house, historic, or somewhere in between?"

"I don't know." He used the handle to raise the lid on the grill.

"Okay, let's go at this from a different direction. Dracula or werewolf?"

"What does—"

"Just answer."

"Dracula, but—"

"That means gothic over woodsy nature." Ashley fiddled with the knobs to get the grill to the perfect temperature, speared the steaks, and tossed them on. Marinade dripped; the fire hissed and emitted a smoky, citrus aroma. After handing Caz the barbeque fork, she said, "Turn them when they brown. Burn mine."

Caz nodded. His phone beeped. He read the text message with a frown and jabbed the fork into one of the steaks.

"What? We're needed on set?"

"No, Mum's texting me about her argument with Dad—again."

"Oh. Sorry. I'm so glad my parents get along; that must be really hard." She winced in sympathy, but left him alone. Enough people pried into his personal business. She was here if he wanted to talk. Inside the kitchen, she gathered a couple of cans of soda, iced tea, and water, not knowing what he'd like, and having a Southern need to comfort with food. She put the tray on the table under the umbrella and held up a glass of iced tea, waited for his shudder of rejection before taking a sip of the cold, sweet drink. "It's fun to eat outside. We don't get to in Houston, not with our heat."

"We have the rain, but the temperature's mild."

"Cotton candy or apple tart?"

"Candy."

"What don't you like about the trailer?"

"Noisy, too small, and too many visitors with keys. No privacy."

"Are you firing that Realtor?"

"Absolutely."

***

A lean crew was headed up to Mt. Whitney for a location shoot. They'd be gone about three days, and the remaining crew, Ashley included, would hang back and work in the warehouse. Ashley didn't mind, though. She hoped to spend some time with Dad this weekend, and she needed a break from Caz to get her head back on straight. Caz couldn't be as appealing as she was starting to think.

On the mountain, three bad guys were going to hold Caz's character hostage. After escaping, Caz's character would hike the trail and spend a cold miserable night by the lake. In reality, the cast and crew would stay in climate-controlled cabins so the trip wouldn't be as rough as it sounded, but Ashley shuddered for them. The air thinned in the mountains and the temperature dropped—not pleasant. When she was a kid, Dad had driven her to some of the scenic parks and she'd gotten nosebleeds and dizzy from the altitude. She was better off in LA, which, like Houston, lay much closer to sea level.

She sat in her usual corner, adding more shading to her sketch, and felt eyes on her. Caz. He held a call sheet, and she saw his gaze shift from her to the AD. She sprang up and hurried over. "Don't."

Caz gave her an innocent look.

"Don't," Ashley said. "I'm a sea-level creature."

His perfect mouth twitched.

"No."

Caz turned away and she followed, stepping into his line of vision.

"Look at me, Caz."

He slanted a look at her from the side of his blue-green eyes.

"No," Ashley said, slowly and clearly, leaving no room for misunderstanding.

"Next week is our last week, then shooting wraps."

"Right, so I'll see you next week and after that for several more in postproduction work."

"I need you there."

"I don't like the mountains."

"You didn't say that when we were house hunting."

"Hollywood Hills isn't exactly Mt. Whitney. Besides, I want you to live wherever you want. I don't have to like the location."

Caz hooked an arm around her waist and drew her in. "Please, please come with me?"

Her cell beeped, delaying her refusal. Ashley looked down and read her text message. "Unexpected meeting in New York, back Sunday, Dad."

Her eyes closed.

"Please," Caz whispered.

"Okay."

***

At first, the weather on the mountain didn't seem too cold. The temperature hovered in the forties. Ashley could handle the forties. She wore layers and Powder gave her little square hand-warmer packets; the beads inside heated up and kept her fingers toasty.

"It's only for three days," Powder said. She seemed to be trying to reassure herself. "And they're setting up a heated tent." She pulled a fake-fur wrap tighter around her head. "I'm going to set up my station." Powder hurried up the path. The rocks on either side of her were khaki colored, and large ridges filled with snow lay in the distance. The whole location was beautiful, and other than Powder's distrust of the outdoors, spirits were high.

Ashley drew in a deep breath. The path smelled like plants and fresh air. Sometimes, you don't realize how polluted a city is until you escape it. White snow edging the path sparkled like diamonds in the sunlight. Snow never accumulated like this in Houston. Ashley couldn't stop herself from patting and crunching the toe of her boot into it.

"See, you like the snow," Caz said. "You're playing in it."

Ashley looked up from the white powder covering the toe of her boot and raised her eyebrows. "Just because it's foreign and interesting doesn't mean I like it."

Caz laughed and pulled her close. "Tell me you like it a little."

Ashley tilted her head back and looked at him through her sunglasses. "Maybe a little."

"I'm foreign and interesting. Tell me you like me a little."

"Well, you're foreign."

The AD stood further up the trail, clapping his mittens together, shifting from one foot to the other, sending anxious looks at the sky. He wanted them locked into three days here: no overtime, no going over budget. "Let's get started and get back to Lone Pine."

The nearby town of Lone Pine served as their base camp. Last night the small group had eaten dinner together in its small hotel, forming a new sense of camaraderie and purpose. Ashley hated to admit it, but these might be her favorite three days of shooting.

Ashley honestly thought that—until it started to rain. Forty degrees was very bearable until you got wet. She huddled in the heated tent as soon as the first drops fell, rolling the hand-warmer packet between her fingers like a rosary. Powder huddled by a heater, staring at her black nail polish. She wasn't outdoorsy either.

The actors rotated in for touchups and to get out of the cold. Ashley had seen them all except the star. "Where's Caz?"

One of the actors answered her. "He's in all the scenes, so they're keeping him out there. Filming will slow if he takes a break."

Ashley groaned, grabbed a blanket and a hot chocolate, and headed for the opening to the tent. The relentless rain, pouring off her umbrella in steady streams, and the muddy ground under her heavy boots, made the fifty feet to the shooting area seem much further.

Caz sat, tied up on a log by a fire, his character's face defiant. His huddled shivering didn't look fake.

"Cut," the AD called.

Ashley moved in and carefully placed the cup between his icy, bound hands.

"Thanks." Caz lifted the drink to his mouth. He made a sound of annoyance and twisted the fake restraints off his wrists. The rope fell beside his boots, soaking into the mud.

Ashley lowered beside him.

"I'm all wet," he warned when she scooted close. Holding the umbrella in one hand, she used the other to toss the blanket half around him, half around herself, and huddled into him. His body radiated chill instead of his usual warmth. Ashley slipped her warmed hand underneath the blanket, his two layers of soaked shirts and touched him. His skin felt icy. She flattened her palm.

Caz made a pleased sound and lifted a hand for the umbrella. "Use both hands."

Ashley slid her other arm around him in a hug, certain his affectionate look was more about her warmth than her company. The nearness made the wetness of his clothing seep through her sweater, and she wondered how he stood it.

"I don't want a house in the mountains either," Caz said. "We can just do a day hike sometime."

Ashley grinned against his arm in total agreement. "You should tell the AD you're ready to stop for the day."

"I'm fine." His body shook.

"Okay," the AD said, "We're ready for you, Caz." Caz muttered a cut-off groan in response.

Ashley noted in annoyance that the AD wore a full parka and had someone holding an umbrella over his head. She gave Caz a final pat and lifted away from him. "I'll get a dry blanket and come back."

***

The temperature was falling with each raindrop, and Caz's skin felt even colder when she returned.

Caz said, "I think this is the last shot." His teeth chattered around the words. "They're worried about the condensation on the cameras."

"Here." Ashley took hold of the umbrella and blanket and slid his hand under her sweater. The icy feel of his fingers against her warm waist made her jump. He tried to withdraw his hand, but she pressed it back in place and took his other, placing both against her skin. The blanket slipped, and she grabbed hold before snuggling into him, one arm around him, one hand clutching the blanket and the umbrella.

"The AD suggested I think warm thoughts, like the beach."

"If your hands are the indicator, that's not working."

Caz leaned his head against her shoulder. "I'm glad I made you come out here with me."

"That's not very nice." The pinging rain became harder pounding rain that blew in sideways. The angle made holding the umbrella over their heads almost useless.

"I'm not nice. Tell me something warm to get me through the next shot."

The AD warned, "Five minutes, Caz."

"Hmm, well, you could think about the lodge and a warm cozy corner by the fire."

"Are you sitting by the fire too?"

"I'm sitting by the fire telling a nice guy all about the kissing pentagon."

Caz stiffened and sat up to look at her with bright eyes.

Ashley said, "Too bad you're not nice."

The AD said, "Okay, we're ready. Let's get this last shot over and wrap. The rain at this angle is really getting to the equipment."

Ashley stood, lifting the blanket with her. Caz surprised her by standing too. He leaned forward to whisper in her ear. "Thanks." He pressed his cold lips to her neck and she shivered, but not due to the cold.

***

Sharing a room with Powder meant giving up all claim to counter space. Powder's stash of cosmetics covered the small area, in addition to every other spare surface in the room. For the first time in her life, Ashley went to bed each night slathered in face creams. Her skin looked great in the morning, but not so much at bedtime.

This was their last dinner together on the mountain. Ashley couldn't say she was sorry. The monsoon had killed her momentary lapse into being a girl who enjoyed the outdoors. She checked her watch; thirty minutes to blow out her hair and dress before dinner.

Powder stood at the wood-framed mirror doing her makeup. She wore black leather pants, a leopard-print tank top, and an intent expression.

Not wanting to get in her way, Ashley took the hairdryer into the bedroom. When she finished, she unplugged the dryer, wound up the cord, and put it away. Her time on set made her more careful with cables. Opening the small wardrobe, she snagged a pair of jeans.

"Not so fast," Powder said from the doorway, holding a tube of makeup like a weapon.

"We're on top of a mountain."

"You're dining with one of the hottest guys on the planet. Well, at least that's what the magazines say, not really my type, but anyway, what kind of friend would I be if I let you go out like that?" Powder patted the counter. "Up."

Even though she'd just taken a shower, the steam was already gone from the bathroom due to the dry California air. Ashley hopped up and let Powder start her makeup.

"You can wear one of my skirts," Powder said.

Ashley's eyes widened and Powder smacked her on the leg. "Eyelids down."

After Powder finished with a dusting of shimmer powder, Ashley assessed her new look. She wore far more makeup than she usually wore, very black eyeliner and glam, completely unsuitable for the woods. She liked it, but she'd never be able to duplicate the makeup without looking crazed. "Thanks."

"You're welcome. Now put on those black tights you wore under your jeans. They'll work. Black bra and your black tank too."

Wow, the tank and the tights; she was going to let her layer.

Powder held up a blue and black plaid miniskirt. The hem came to mid-thigh on Ashley, so the skirt must be a micro mini on the tall Powder. It wasn't much of a layer.

Powder said, "We need to go shopping together when we get back."

"Cool." Ashley grabbed her black pullover; the sweater still felt damp under her fingers.

"Ack, don't, what are you doing?"

"Um, it's forty degrees."

"That thing got all wet."

"My other one got really dirty when I slid on the trail."

Powder shook her head. "And you wonder why you couldn't catch that guy back home. What are they teaching you girls in Texas?"

"I will freeze if I go down there like this. I'm wearing a tank top and a mini skirt and its freezing."

"Please, if some guy doesn't step up to offer you his jacket or a warm arm around your shoulder within five minutes, I'll go without makeup all week."

Ashley gasped. "Really?"

"No. But trust me, you'll thank me later."

"I only have the hiking boots."

"They kind of work."

***

With that approval, Ashley walked down the main stairs of the lodge, arm in arm with Powder, braced to hear any crap about her outfit.

The bar area was almost full tonight. A few of the crew sat in overstuffed armchairs scattered around the room, but most stood belly up to the bar. Arms waved and Powder gravitated toward them.

The promised warmth of the fireplace's golden flames drew Ashley in the other direction. The popping crackles of the wood underscored the country music coming out of the corner jukebox, and the burning log smelled like it was from a real tree instead of a ceramic fake. Ashley breathed in the realness, so different from being on set, and lowered herself to the hearth with a hand against the rough bricks. She hoped the bricks wouldn't snag Powder's skirt, but she wasn't willing to relinquish the position of the fire even if they did. The fire heated the skin of her bare shoulders, and she shifted, trying to expose as much skin as possible to the flames. Any part of her not directly in front of the fire chilled, so she had to keep up the rotation. She sat alone for about one minute.

A male voice said, "Can I get you a drink?"

Ashley turned away from the hypnotic orange glow to look up at the guy. He looked college-aged, and had a love of the outdoors. The flannel gave that away.

"Oh, no, I'm good, thanks."

"That was killer rain today. Seriously." He took a sip of his beer.

Before she could answer, another guy joined them wearing a UCLA sweatshirt. "Dude, my trail was mashed up."

Ashley couldn't decide if her sudden popularity was because there weren't many girls in the room or her proximity to the fireplace.

Powder returned from the bar holding two pink drinks. She handed one to Ashley and winked at the nearest guy. "Yep, definitely a day to stay inside."

Ashley swiveled the glass in her hand, wishing the drink was heated. "Thanks. Uh, what is it?"

"It's called a Rain Ender," Powder said.

Ashley smiled at the made-up name and put the chilled glass to her lips. Sweet and tart with a kick. The Rain Ender was juice and something alcoholic. She moved the glass away from the flames, holding the stem against her knees.

The UCLA guy said, "Dude, we're going to need another round of those."

Powder looked him up and down. "You're on the water polo team and you can't handle a little water?"

Ashley was impressed. She hadn't realized his sweatshirt was for the water polo team. Powder had moves. She took another drink.

Flannel guy snickered and took a seat by Ashley. Eyeing his warm shirt with a little envy, she watched goose bumps appear on her arm as she raised her glass.

He said, "You go to school around here?"

"No," Ashley said. "I'm only here for the summer. I'm going to college in Texas next fall."

"Have you toured UCLA yet? I could show you around."

"It's on my to-do list. What's your major?"

"Urban design."

"No way."

"Way."

Ashley said, "I'm going to be an architect, too."

"Really?" The flannel guy looked pleased as he held out a hand. "I'm Scott."

"Ashley." She took his calloused hand and shook it. Scott seemed reluctant to let go when she pulled back. Her only reluctance was that his hand was warm.

"So what's your interest? Building restoration, new design, community planning?"

"Mmm, I don't know enough about them to say for certain, but probably new design."

"That's what I thought when I was a freshman, but I totally changed after a few classes, so you should keep your mind open to the possibilities."

"She knows her mind pretty well." A British voice joined the group.

Ashley smiled up at Caz and held up her free hand.

His return smile was brooding as he took in her outfit. She braced for a smart remark, but he didn't deliver one. He took her hand and squeezed in beside her then said, "When we went house hunting, she knew exactly what she liked."

Scott's smile wavered.

Ashley sent Caz a quizzical look. He made it sound like they were moving in together. Was he trying to add to the gossip? Whatever. He looked warm in his big cozy sweater. She leaned back against him and breathed in. The soap he used had some type of woodsy tone, different from his usual stuff, still nice, though.

"Well, like I said, she should keep her options open." Scott rose from his seat on the fireplace then bent down and clicked his beer against her glass. "I'm Scott Parrnelli. Find me in the student directory if you want that tour." With those words, he walked away, back toward the bar.

Caz said, "The crew is going into dinner."

"Okay." Ashley stood, then looked at Powder and her water polo player.

"I'll hang out here for a while," Powder said. "You two go ahead."

Caz took Ashley's hand and led her down the hall past the row of stuffed animal heads. "Where's the rest of your clothes?"

"I thought you were going to be nice tonight."

"Nope."

"Well, my sweater got wet helping out a friend. So it's drying. My other jacket got dirty the first day on the trail. I thought two would be enough. Guess not."

"Powder didn't have anything?"

"I'm wearing her skirt."

That drew his eyes down to her legs. Ashley stopped his words before they could form. "Powder said some nice guy would probably lend me his flannel shirt. I had a pretty good shot at it too, until you walked up."

Caz sighed, reached down, and pulled his white cable-knit sweater over his head. Underneath he wore a cream-colored long-sleeved T-shirt.

Ashley grinned and held up her arms. “Touchdown.”

Caz dropped the hem over her head. “That’s an American reference.”

She pulled her arms through, the knit still warm from his body. The material fell almost to the hem of her skirt, and she hugged it close. “You understood well enough. Mmm. Nice, thanks.”

Caz pulled her hair free of the collar and patted the length down her back. Instead of joining the crew at a picnic-style table, he led her to a corner table for two.

The restaurant’s food choices centered around wild game, but in this cold, there was no contest. They both ordered the hot potato soup. Eyeing him over the rim of her spoon, Ashley blew to cool it and took a bite, eating a creamy square of potato.

“I thought over dinner you could tell me about the kissing pentagon.”

CHAPTER 15

Her spoon dropped back into the soup, and the handle made a small clatter against the side of the dish.

Caz gave his sweater a sweeping nod. "You said if I was nice."

"Is it really a nice gesture, if you do it to get a reward?"

"Yes." Caz leaned closer. "So, you'd call the kissing pentagon a reward?"

Smiling around her next bite, Ashley nodded.

"Intriguing. Will I call it a reward?"

Ashley considered. "Maybe, I don't know what you like. But the kissing pentagon doesn't involve rain."

"They didn't create the technique in Britain then."

Her gaze caught sight of Jason, wearing one of his button-down shirts under a full navy sweater, leading Powder by the arm. He seemed annoyed, and Powder seemed satisfied. That would teach Jason to be late. Poor UCLA guy. Ashley wondered what the water polo equivalent of a strikeout was called.

Caz tapped his spoon on the side of the bowl and drew her attention to him.

Ashley said, "It's kind of cool that no one here recognizes you."

"The eight layers and coats with hoods help."

"You'll have to vacation in Alaska," Ashley said. "Freedom from photos."

"Or maybe it's because there's mostly guys here," Caz said. "They don't scream as much as the women."

Ashley rolled her eyes.

"That guy was being quite forward," Caz said. "He fancied you."

"You call that forward?"

"He asked you out when you're clearly with me."

Ashley didn't let her happy reaction to his words show. "Well, he didn't take any of his clothes off and throw them at me, like women do to you."

"I inspire passion."

"I should do womankind a favor and keep the kissing pentagon a secret. That knowledge, coupled with your already irresistible self, would be too much of an advantage."

Caz finished his soup and pushed the bowl away. "Tomorrow there could be more rain, or bears, or an earthquake. We have to grab the chance at life while we can."

"Really? You're giving me the *we may not make it out of here alive* speech?" She took another bite and stirred her soup.

"Is it working?"

"A little. I don't like earthquakes." Ashley let the spoon drop and leaned close. "The technique works better as a demo than a speech."

"Yes, show me." Caz popped to his feet, eyes bright, and pulled her up from the table. They looked in the bar area but it was still packed. Caz led her to the front door. "Wait here one second, I'll be right back." He returned within a few minutes carrying a large coat.

Coats and front doors meant one thing. "No way. The weather's too cold and damp."

"You have on a sweater."

"But I'm wearing a skirt."

Caz shrugged on the coat. "How long is the pentagon's first step?"

"Not that long." Ashley looked toward the crowded, well-lit interior and toward the exit. "Okay."

Caz opened the door and they slipped outside. The cold hit them instantly. It was a damp cold because of the rain, a Houston kind of cold. Brr.

Caz led her over to the side of the lodge, away from the bright front entry lights.

Shivering, Ashley reached for him. The building only blocked a little of the bitter breeze. He was going to have to serve as the other barrier if he wanted her to stay out here much longer. Caz wrapped his arms around her and she backed up until she felt the log cabin's wall at her back. "You know what would be great?"

"Hmm?"

"If we do this back in LA. Picture your cozy trailer, or even my car in the parking lot. That's very American, you know, so you should experience that—making out in a car."

"Okay, yes," he agreed. "But now show me step one."

Ashley heart thumped and she felt a little less cold. She tilted her head back against the log and looked up. He was kind of tall to demonstrate the first step on, unless they had a chair.

The night was pitch-black around them, lit only by the lights from the hotel and the ton of stars in the sky, their sheer numbers and brightness something never seen in LA. The difference highlighted how unreal the night felt. She lifted her gaze to his face, but couldn't really read his expression in the dark. "Powder told me the steps, but didn't say anything about conditions. I don't know if the techniques work out here in the cold."

"Jeez, now I have to know."

She gave a small laugh. "Okay, I have to reach your mouth to do this."

"So far it doesn't sound that unique."

"You're awfully talkative for someone who wants to learn something."

"That's because I like it when you say nice things about my voice." Leaning down, Caz tilted his head toward hers.

Ashley rose on her tiptoes, then saw a better option and pulled back. "Hey, see that? What is it? An arbor?"

Caz turned his head. A rustic wooden structure stood in the darkness, not too far away. "No, I think it's for people who want to sleep outside."

"When there's a lodge thirty feet away?" Disbelief colored her voice.

He shrugged. "Let's check it out." The camping structure had a wooden platform about two feet off the ground, three wooden walls, and a missing fourth wall.

Caz said, "Look at this, there's a whole bit missing."

"They left it off on purpose, so you can enjoy the view."

"Of the bears?"

"Again, I'm with you. Climb in. You'll be like those first British explorers who came to America under rough conditions."

"My people stayed in England." Caz climbed in and gave her a hand up. The inside was dark, and much less chilly without the wind. Leaning against the wall, he pulled her close.

"You're tall."

Caz slid down the wall to the floor and pulled her down onto his lap. After opening his coat, he pulled her close. The wooden floor was cold against her knees and her tights were definitely getting snagged, but he was warm.

"Mmm. Okay. You start with this—"

Ashley kissed his mouth, a soft, fleeting touch. He pressed upwards and she pulled back, not letting him reach her. "This one's all about being frustrated."

She couldn't clearly see him, but she could hear the grin in his words. "Ashley, that's never the goal."

She kissed the other corner of his grin then pressed her lips lightly to his bottom lip.

"Caz." Next, she touched her tongue to his mouth and pulled back. "I like how you taste. Kind of foreign and exciting. It's too dark out here to see, but sometimes when I kiss you your eyes darken and—"

Caz grabbed her and kissed her passionately on the mouth; he totally skipped step one, and she didn't care. Nudging her mouth open with his, he took charge. Her mind went blank and her body tingled. Caz raised the sweater up and over her head.

Ashley wasn't cold anymore. She moved closer, shoved his jacket off, and pressed against his hard chest. He put an arm to the floor and stood. Her boots thumped to the floor. He grabbed her and lifted her. Feeling weightless, she wrapped her legs around his waist and her arms around his neck. He moved a step forward, bracing her against the wall. For a second she felt the wall against her back, then the firmness of him, then a feeling of weightlessness.

Weightlessness, falling, bam. Her arm hit something hard and her body landed against Caz. Evidently, the three-sided walls weren't connected. They'd fallen through a gap, off the platform and onto the ground. Ashley tried to suck in a breath, but it took a second. With a groan she lifted off of Caz. "You okay?"

He groaned. "No."

"Want to go inside?"

"Yes."

Standing, Ashley brushed at her clothes in order to brush off nature. Her fingertips felt tight from the cold. Dry, powdery snow dusted her arms. She couldn't see her sweater or the jacket in the darkness; if they were still on the platform, she had no interest in climbing back up to get them.

Ashley moved toward the lodge. Wind whipped through night, sticks crackled underneath her boots, and she clutched her arms to her chest. Every frozen step brought her closer to the porch and the light. First the path became visible, then the steps. Warmth was close. Ashley jogged the last few feet and slipped into the welcome warmth of the foyer, holding the door for Caz.

The light of the foyer shined, revealing his mussed hair, flushed face, and bits of nature clinging to him—dirt, leaves, snow. When nature attacked, nature won.

***

They had shot the final scenes back in warehouse 47 and the wrap party was tomorrow night. While glad the film was finished, Ashley couldn't believe Caz hadn't said anything about them going together. He'd spent most of the day staring at his phone. Maybe she misread things and she was just a convenient work friend in his mind.

Garrett wasn't as preoccupied as Caz. He still had time to talk to her. The supporting actor grinned, his Scottish accent as pronounced as ever. "Going to the wrap party? There's going to be food. The darling in craft services said they'd be using an outside caterer."

"Thank God. I won't have to eat first."

"I'll still eat first." Garrett patted his flat stomach. "Then go for a run, and eat there too. Save a dance for me."

Someone didn't mind making plans in advance.

***

The studio had rented a private room off the main dance floor in a country-western themed bar. The place smelled like spilled beer and hay overlaid with fog from the fog machine. The cast, crew, and their dates packed the place. The vibe of the room was excitement. Filming was done.

Everyone wore country-influenced clothes except Garrett. He wore his blue and green kilt. "Hey, Ashley. Dance?" Garrett pulled her onto the dance floor. He was too tall for her, but Garrett did a mean waltz, and he ended it with a dip so deep her head nearly touched the floor. When she lifted her eyes, her gaze met Caz's glare.

Caz stood on the sidelines with Petra beside him, whispering in his ear.

So, Caz came after all. Ashley looked back to Garrett. "Thanks for the dance."

"We'll have to try it again, darling." Garrett released her hands slowly. "Or we could grab a bite to eat? They have a snack area. It's just miniatures, though, but I saw chocolate puffs."

Ashley smiled noncommittally and took the time-honored easy way out. She scooted around him, off a side exit, and entered the women's room.

Olive stood inside, dressed in denim, replacing the lid on a small pill bottle. "Headache." Olive tightened the lid. "Because I work so much." She stomped out.

Grateful Olive hadn't asked for a temple rub, Ashley used the facilities, washed up, and went to the door. After she left the restroom, Garrett caught up to her again. "This is a great wrap party, reminds me of Hogmanay in Edinburgh."

"What's that?"

Before Garrett could answer, Olive scooted around him and handed a drink to Ashley. "Here, Caz requested this. I'd take it but you know how he is."

Ashley looked at the glass. Really? Work was over and she was still expected to carry Caz's drinks? Garrett reached for the glass, but Ashley had her own agenda. She moved away. "I got this." She took the drink to Caz, ignored Olive who followed her and Petra who stood too close to him. She thrust the glass against his chest.

Caz smiled at her and wrapped his fingers over hers. "Thanks."

Ashley wiggled her hand free.

Petra coughed and scooted even closer. "And my audition went like this." She grabbed the air and rocked side to side. Diamonds sparkled on each of her fingers, and the fringe on her tight white suede cowgirl dress danced with each exaggerated gesture. The rhinestones on her matching white boots flashed with her accompanying stomps. "The part is a bikini-wearing ski instructor who is half mermaid, and she saves her students from Ukrainian bad guys." Petra dropped her hands to her small waist and grinned. "I won the most coveted part in Hollywood. I start shooting next week."

"The most coveted," Olive said. "You'll look great in an ocean film."

"I know. And it's shooting here in LA." Petra squealed. "No out of town, out of touch for me. I'll be here, where I can be around all the great shops and industry people."

Caz said, "You don't want a break?"

Petra widened her eyes and twisted her mouth. While shaking her head, she caught sight of the AD. "Yoo-hoo, have I told you—" Petra chased after him.

Caz looked at Ashley. "Dance with me."

"No."

Caz took a drink. "Please?"

"Maybe."

"I want you to." Caz downed the drink, then set the glass on a nearby table. He grabbed her hand and tugged her out onto the dance floor.

As they weaved through the couples, Ashley said, "How much have you had to drink?"

Caz peered at her through glassy eyes from beneath his untidy hair. "One."

Once they were in the middle of the floor, Caz positioned Ashley in front of him, took a step toward her, ran two hands down the side of her hair, and stepped back. It was unlike any two-step she'd ever done. She couldn't tell if he danced this way because he was European, or drunk, or both, but his movements were weird.

"That's not how you two-step."

Caz moved closer and danced to the left. "Why were you dancing with him?" He glared at Garrett.

She ignored the question, concentrating on his continued misinterpretation of the country and western dance. "I'll show you how." Ashley took his left hand with her right one and held it up.

Caz looked at the paired couples circling the dance floor around them. He placed his right hand against the back of her blue silk camisole and pulled her close. She put her left hand on his shoulder and pushed back a bit. Caz resisted her attempts to lead and they ended up in a type of junior-high clench, his arms around her waist, hers around his neck. Her boots saved her feet from his missed steps.

The position actually worked nicely as the song changed into the movie's romantic theme, "Love's Romantic Ruin." The lights dimmed even darker and ceiling disco balls rotated, creating circles of light that highlighted their steps on the dance floor. "Our song," Caz said.

Ashley relaxed in his arms.

He slid one hand against her jean-clad hips and one around her waist. He bent his head toward her. "I'm not having it," his deep voice said into her ear. Then he jerked his head toward Garrett.

"It's cute that you think you get an opinion," Ashley said.

"You're *my* assistant."

"We've discussed this. No, I'm not." She'd seen her fair share of party drunks back home. It wasn't an attractive look as a rule.

Caz pulled her close to him and spoke intently in French as if she could understand. She could only catch one in four words, thanks to last year's French Two. There was a big difference between slow and clear classroom French and actual conversational French. "You know I can't understand you, right?"

Caz moved even closer and brushed a hand against her hair, then said something insistently. Ashley smiled and let him talk. He paused and looked at her expectantly.

"You know I can't understand half of that."

Caz tilted his head down and kissed her. Her eyes closed and she leaned into him. He pulled away and spoke into her ear. "Mine."

Ashley melted.

"My assistant, not Garrett's."

Oh. "I'm not your assistant anymore."

"You aren't Garrett's."

"I was never Garrett's." Ashley spoke slowly with firm words. "I was never yours."

"Garrett asked you out."

"And?" Ashley didn't bother to explain that Garrett had no interest in her. His weakness may be girls, but his interest in Ashley extended only as far as it would irritate Caz.

Caz frowned. He slid an arm from her waist, threaded a hand through her hair, and played idly with the strands. "What do you think of the song?"

"It's beautiful."

Looking into his eyes, she saw a glint of something. She closed her eyes against it and leaned into him.

His arms tightened around her. "Yeah."

Ashley felt his body stiffen and looked up. His gaze was beside her.

Garrett stood a step away tapping on Caz's shoulder. "May I cut in? Darling PA looks so sweet tonight, I really can't resist."

Did Garrett even know her name or did he call every girl *darling*?

Caz's body stiffened further, and she could clearly read his expression then—pissed drunk.

Caz released her and turned toward Garrett.

Spitting something out in French, Caz took an aggressive step closer to his ex-best friend.

CHAPTER 16

Ashley couldn't understand the words, but Garrett must've. He stiffened, his fists clenched, and he said, "Get over it already." Then he shoved Caz in the shoulder.

Caz threw the first punch. Garrett barreled back into him, and they hit the dance floor.

"Stop it!" Ashley yelled.

Couples scurried out of their path, and a flash went off behind them.

The big men shoved against each other, elbows, fists, and knees flying. It was a good thing Caz had martial arts training because as big as he was, Garrett was bigger. Another flash lit across the fight.

Paparazzi. They were near and they had cameras. A drunken brawl was the last thing Caz needed.

Boomer grabbed Garrett and pulled him up. Garrett strained against his hold, but Boomer looped his arms through Garrett's, immobilizing him. Garrett threw his head back and popped Boomer in the face with the back of his skull. Boomer's arms dropped and his hand cupped his nose to stop the gushing red blood.

Garrett reached for Caz, still on the floor.

Caz lashed out, catching Garrett in the thigh with a vicious kick. Garrett stumbled back a step. The next flash lit up Garrett's face. He stopped, blinked, and turned away from the camera. He mumbled something about "not here" and retreated.

Caz got to his feet, eyes tracking Garrett.

Ashley grabbed his elbow and shook it. He weaved a little.

"Caz."

No response.

"Caz. Stop it." She slid one hand over his jaw so she could tilt his head toward her. "Reporters. We need to get out." She shook his arm again. Caz resisted, blinked, then looked down at her with an unfocused expression.

Ashley took his hand. "Reporters. Come with me." Leading him through the other dancers, past the restrooms, toward the back exit she'd seen earlier, Ashley hurried down a narrow corridor. Boxes of liquor were stacked in crates along the wall and the smell of beer was even stronger here. More flashes hit them. Crossing her fingers that an alarm wouldn't sound, Ashley shoved into the exit bar on the door and pulled Caz out behind her. The exit door slammed shut.

The back lot was dark, lit only by a streetlamp a few feet from the Dumpster. Ashley hesitated a moment, uncertain where the drivers were parked, and looked back to the bar. The exit door didn't have a handle on this side, so no returning. She bit her lip in indecision.

The glow of a cigarette off to the right clued her in to the drivers taking a cigarette break. Next, she spotted the Jaguar. Ashley pointed, but Caz, slumped against the wall, didn't look up from the screen on his cell phone.

"Wait here," she said in a firm voice that couldn't be misunderstood by the drunkest of partiers. She ran to the Jaguar. Her boots crunched against a broken beer bottle when she took her eyes off the ground to wave at the driver. "We have to go." She kicked against the glass and threw herself into the back of the limo.

The driver stomped out his cigarette, and by the time the Jaguar crawled onto the street and got near enough to Caz, the paparazzi had surrounded him. Ashley flung open the door, then ducked back against gray leather seat. Caz struggled through the reporters and to the limo, landing inside with a pinched expression. "They—"

Caz's phone beeped. "It's from my mum." He read his text message out loud with a voice full of sarcasm and heavy with a British accent. "It's going to be different this time. When your film wraps, I want you to have dinner with your father and me."

"They're together again?"

He glared down at his phone. "Sure." The speaker rang under his stare and he swiped a clumsy finger at the answer key, and put the receiver to his ear.

Ashley heard only his part of the conversation. "No…When?...You're wrong." Caz hung up and grabbed her black evening purse from the seat. Before she could stop him, he unzipped it and dumped the contents on the seat.

A small prescription bottle fell out amid the rest of her stuff: wallet, keys, lipstick.

"Why are you in my purse? Give it."

Caz tossed the small purse back to her and clutched the bottle in both hands, staring at it.

The pill bottle wasn't hers, but she'd seen one like it in the women's room earlier this evening—Olive's headache pills. "How weird, what are those—"

"Why do you have these?" The beep on his phone distracted him. "It's my agent," he said then read aloud, "Online press have you slumped in alley behind club. Meet me about damage control." The phone beeped again and Caz read the second text. "You lost the part in a Moliere because of your insistence on a vacation." He flung it, and the phone clattered against the wall.

Ashley watched his loss of control with shock. This was not like him at all.

Caz jabbed a hand toward the window. "The press is out there."

"Okay," Ashley said, confused. He was all over the place.

"You told them."

"Told them what?"

"That I'm here."

"What?"

"You told the press where I'd be."

"No. Why would you say that?"

"Make me understand," Caz said. "You say you want to be an architect, but you're interning on a movie."

"I like movies. It doesn't mean I want to do this for a living. I want a job on my college applications, an interesting one. Marissa's going to be a chef, and she works at the Fry Hut. It's what we normal teenagers do. Get a summer job."

"Yet somehow you're actually on film."

"The back of me, in a wig, and it'll probably be cut. I've done background before. Scenes get cut."

"You admit it. You've done this before."

"Yeah. Once, when I was little, I sat on a bench as part of the background. Big deal."

"Stop lying." Caz leaned forward, his hands against the edge of the seat. "I'm in this business. I don't care if you want to be famous. If you want a career, just be honest."

Ashley's mouth fell open and she stared at him. Shaking her head, she didn't know what to say.

"You sought attention from the first day. You ended up in my car. You ended up on my set."

"This movie began filming during my visit with my dad. Did I arrange that too? Ask them to hold shooting until it was time for my summer break?"

Caz ignored her words.

"Then you gave me that sexy gift," Caz said. "You got my attention."

"No. I was being nice. You *know* what I heard."

"I don't know, you never told me. And you weren't that nice. We never opened the box."

She was a happy, nonviolent person who now wanted to throw something at his stupid head. "What is this about? Why are you so mad at me?"

"Petra told me." Caz slurred her name. "She called me because she's worried." He jerked a hand toward his discarded phone.

"Told you what?"

He shook the pill bottle and glared. "What's in this? This bottle?"

"Pills, they're—"

He didn't give her time to finish. Throwing the pill bottle onto the floor, he said, "Yours."

"No. What did Petra tell you?"

"She saw you with the bottle." Caz pointed at the small prescription bottle. "And I found 'em. You didn't hide the bottle very well. It was in your bag."

Ashley gasped. "Petra said she saw me with Olive's headache pills?"

"You acted so innocent, like you were trying to help me. When you're the one who used them on me, and she also saw you with Garrett. Everyone saw you with Garrett." His words were a crazy mix of slurred paranoia and accusation.

Ashley shook her head. "Why would I give you one of Olive's migraine pills?" She lifted the bottle from the floor and stared at a label that had no meaning to her. She guessed they were Olives. "What are these?"

"Those aren't for headaches." Caz bit the words out between clenched teeth. "Petra thinks you gave them to Lorene too, so you could take her part."

Ashley gasped. "You think someone drugged Lorene when she came to the set? I thought she was drunk."

"She was, but maybe she was something more. Petra thinks so."

"I didn't do this, whatever it is you're accusing me of. Why would you believe Petra over me?"

Caz slid away. "I've worked with Petra for years. She's a pain, but she doesn't use or lie."

Ashley leaned closer. "I didn't. I got you out of that party, away from the press."

"The press was waiting for us. And why were you with Garrett?"

"I wasn't. You're not listening to me. You know me, why are you acting like this?"

"I thought I knew you. Of course, I thought I knew my best friend."

"Wait." Ashley put a hand on his arm, "I am not like Garrett; I'm not an actor."

"You're a liar like him, and I'm not my mother. I'm not going to keep taking you back no matter how bad the crap gets."

"Take me back? Your mother? What are you talking about now?" Nothing he said made sense.

"Admit it."

"You know what I admit?"

He stilled, and she looked directly in his face, her eyes burning. "I admit I knew better than to hang out with Hollywood types. You're overdramatic. You create problems where they don't exist. And I'm not having this fight while you're drunk."

"I had one drink, and then the one you gave me. Petra said you put something in it." He repeated the accusation and his accent got heavier and his words slurred the more he talked.

Ashley waved a hand toward the window. "I'd never drug anyone. You must like all the attention. You're the actor. You probably called the press."

Caz glared in response.

Ashley shook her head at him. "I'll make it easy. You're right. Believe Petra."

The car drew to a stop in front of dad's gate. Ashley unlocked the handle before stepping out. "And by the way, no one's perfect. You should forgive Garrett. If no one can make a mistake around you, you're going to be pretty lonely." Ashley slammed her way out of the limo, shutting off the spew of French.

***

Ashley awakened the next day thinking about Caz, knowing she should have explained better, and made sure he was okay. She rolled out of bed, went for her purse, and dumped it out. The phone rolled onto the beige carpet beside her bare feet.

No messages.

Holding tight to the phone, she dialed Caz. He didn't pick up and she hung up on his outgoing voice message. Ashley stared at the screen a moment then crawled back into the warm sheets. Hugging a pillow to her chest, she went over everything they'd said. With each replay, she thought of how to explain better and what she should have said. Surely, he'd find out the truth and call. She set the phone on her nightstand, trying to compose the perfect message in her mind before dialing again.

A picture of her parents rested on the bedside table. They looked young, scared, and happy in that photo. She reached for her phone again, but grabbed the silver picture frame instead. The love on Mom's face was painful. Her parents loved each other, but couldn't stay married. Mom was like her: normal, happy. Dad was drama. He worked in it and thrived on upheaval. They had divorced soon after she was born. Sharing a child was an incredible reason to try to stay together, but they knew better. They weren't compatible.

On set, the process was interesting and exciting, but she really didn't get it. She had no desire to share her private thoughts with everyone. Film people made exciting friends, but you didn't date them.

She should never have tried with Caz. She knew better. Caz didn't trust her and had created this whole fight out of nothing. This was his life. For heaven's sake, he was an actor.

Ashley sat up. What was she thinking? Being with Caz would never work. Not that he'd even asked for a relationship. She put the frame down and scrambled out of bed, her heart racing, her mind clear. Caz didn't need another explanation. She just needed to finish her postproduction work, get this job on her college applications, and in three weeks, go home to the real world.

***

Twenty people sat in the conference room. The only people she recognized were the actors and the assistants. The rest of the postproduction team was new to her.

She and Olive had sat in chairs against the wall, and the key players sat at a conference table. The AD went over scheduling and the postproduction plans. She couldn't help looking at Caz a couple of times during the speech but he wouldn't meet her gaze. Olive threw speculative looks between them, but Ashley didn't volunteer any information.

The director gave his welcome and then turned the meeting back over to the AD. When the director slipped from the room in the middle of the AD's speech, Caz got up and followed him. On his way past her chair, he pointed for Ashley to follow.

Great, so this was how it's going to be? He didn't even call her *PA*. He was going to point from now on?

When she reached the corridor, Caz was speaking in a low, intense voice to the director. His arms were crossed over his chest, his feet braced apart. The director held his hands out, palms up.

She reached them in time to hear the last bit of Caz's sentence.

"It's either her or me."

Ashley's face flooded with heat and her stomach churned.

"Caz, she's one of the interns who goes back to school in a few weeks. We'll assign her to another department."

"I work with all the departments, but I won't if she's there."

Ashley's mouth opened then closed without words, and she swallowed against her knotting stomach.

The director looked up. "This is why I said no hookups." He dropped his gaze to her. "You've done a good job, but we can't replace Caz. We'll put you on another production for the rest of your time."

Ashley backed up and her voice came out high. "No need, I'm going home." Eyes burning, she turned away from them. She wanted to walk out with her head held high, walking slow and proud, but her pace quickened with each step.

Caz had gotten her fired. Now she couldn't put this job on her college applications. She'd have to tell her mom she got fired, and she'd have to tell Marissa, then she'd have to get a job at the Fry Hut. By the time she reached Dad's building, she was running. She took the elevator up, rushed straight past his secretary, and reached for his doorknob.

"Ashley, sorry, dear," his secretary said, "Your dad won't be back from Zurich until Friday. He's already left for the airport."

Ashley stared at the dark wood of the door for several seconds. Dad hadn't said he was going out of town. He'd left the country and hadn't bothered to tell her.

"Are you all right, dear?"

Choked up, she couldn't speak, so she waved off his secretary's concern and left for the ladies' room. She ran her hands under the cool water in the faucet, trying to calm down. Her stressed blue eyes stared back at her in the mirror. She splashed cold water on her hot cheeks. It didn't help.

Ashley gave up trying to go unnoticed and ran out.

It was time to go home.

CHAPTER 17

Senior year. Everything looked the same but felt different. It amazed Ashley that she could spend the summers running around million-dollar movie sets, but one month later and she couldn't be trusted to stand in the hall after the bell rang.

Ashley turned to her best friend. "Can senioritis hit as early as September?"

Marissa's groan of "yes" held all the weight of twelve years of oppression. She unlatched her locker and snagged an emerald sweater off the hook. The sweater was her favorite and the bright color matched her eyes.

Ashley said. "Did you wear that sweater to work?"

Marissa sniffed the sleeve. "Why? Does it smell like fries?"

"Yep."

Marissa shrugged. "French class is too cold." She continued muttering, but switched to French and went on about fries and the weather.

Hearing French made her think of Caz. Missing him, and being angry with him, was taking up a ridiculous amount of her time and she couldn't seem to make her thoughts stop. Last night at the grocery store, she'd caught herself scouring the tabloids. That was how far she'd fallen and how desperate she was for news about him. Even knowing the stories were probably untrue, Ashley hated the pictures of him with other girls. And there was lots to hate because there were lots of pictures, fans, models, and actresses.

Ashley didn't talk much about her own summer, but Marissa's nemesis and part-time Fry Hut Manager, Irina, did, not the Fry Hut Manager part, but about her August in Italy. All her conversations started with, "In Italia we," or "The Italians would,' or "That's wrong because in Roma..."

Marissa usually followed with, "Well, at the Fry Hut we..." or "Did you go to Italy?"

Ashley's cell phone beeped, a text message from Dad: "Back from trip. Have you headed back to school?"

Ashley pressed her lips together, wishing she could find the words funny, but she knew her eyes were burning when she put her phone away without replying. She'd been in Texas for a couple of weeks now.

***

By November, Ashley didn't want any news or any reminder of Caz. He could forget her? Fine. She could forget him. Of course, that was the week the movie's theme song, "Love's Romantic Ruin," became popular on the radio. Ashley couldn't go down the halls or turn on her stereo without hearing someone sing the lyrics.

Marissa appeared beside her, interrupting her thoughts, which was good since she should've been working on her college application essays. She needed one more referral.

Marissa poked her in the arm until she looked up. Her face was flushed, her emerald eyes bright.

"What?"

"You've got to see this."

Marissa held up her phone and said, "The movie preview. You're totally in it."

Ashley dropped her gaze to the screen and the trailer for *Eternal Loss, Eternal Revenge* came on. The clip was short and the narration made her heart stop. Caz's voice came through the speakers. It had been so long since she'd heard him. She even knew the words his character was saying since she'd been in the recording studio when he'd recorded them.

The trailer opened with a visual of Caz's haunted eyes staring out, and his British voice continued through the speakers.

"Drinking, women, risks, I tried them all and nothing made me forget the pain." The camera angle widened, and behind Caz was Ashley, dressed in a pale sundress, her hand reaching for a car door handle. Before touching it, she looked back and gifted him a sweet smile. Then an explosion lit the screen, and you knew she was gone.

Caz's voice went husky. "I can't forget." The clip ended, and Caz said the final words: "It's time to give them something to remember."

Ashley's breath left her lungs. Wow. That was her smile. She'd washed that car on the set. She'd done Caz's eyeliner. That was her in the wig. Her total screen time was probably one second, but it was her.

"So what, do you want to be an actress now?" Marissa said with enthusiasm.

"No, architecture's still it for me."

Marissa squeezed her arm. "One day, I'll text you a picture of a building you designed."

***

Ashley and her mom searched the racks at the department store, looking for a dress. Ashley held up an ice-blue one. "What do you think?"

A frown slid off Mom's face. "You'll look beautiful in anything."

Ashley smiled. Powder would not agree. She'd have to send her some pictures and get her input. When Powder had stayed in touch by reaching out with a text, Ashley had been glad. She'd asked the makeup artist her real name, and Powder had texted back that she wasn't saying. Evidently, it was worse than *Powder*.

Mom worried at her lip and her voice was soft and low. "Um, Ashley?"

"Yeah?" Ashley slid hangers further down the metal rack, looking for her size.

"Um, well, I know you don't have a date, but sometimes that doesn't mean you won't meet someone at the dance. You know about condoms, right?"

"Mom!" Ashley stopped sorting and looked up. "I'm not sleeping with anyone." As she said the words, she wondered why the thought of sleeping with one of the guys at her high school was so appalling. There were some hot guys at THS.

"It's only that, things happen, and you don't always mean them to, and you need to be prepared."

Ashley continued her search, keeping her eyes on the clothes instead of her mom's bright red face. "I know you had me in college, so I wasn't exactly planned."

Mom wrapped her arms around her waist. "It's not that. You were my favorite gift ever. Just —"

Ashley shook her head. "Mom, really, we don't have to go there."

***

"Dad sent a package," Mom said, as Ashley climbed the stairs. "I put it on your bed."

"Thanks." Ashley opened the door and dropped her backpack inside.

On her bed lay a cream-colored envelope atop three huge dress boxes. She slid the flap out and removed an embossed card. "You are hereby invited to the worldwide premiere of *Eternal Loss, Eternal Revenge."*

Ashley sank down on her bed. Folded behind the card was a travel itinerary detailing a flight booked in her name from Houston's Intercontinental Airport direct to LAX. She let the papers drop and stood to open the three dress boxes. A flowing white gown lay in one, a sleek red one in another and a black sophisticated one in the third. She touched the delicate fabric of the white one. Could she go? Did they let fired people in? Pressing the heel of her hand against her forehead, she wrapped her free arm around her waist. She should've told Dad she was fired from the project.

Screw that. She'd worked hard on the film and wanted to see it. She didn't want to be stuck at home while Caz worked the red carpet like he was the only one who'd worked on the film. Who cared if Caz believed her or not? All the drama, mixed in with ego, and all the problems that actors created for themselves. He was Hollywood dressed in a British accent.

Her ringtone sounded and the screen showed a picture of Marissa. She tried to sound normal when she answered. "Hello?"

"I found my dress. It's awesome," Marissa said. "Kind of an eggplant color. I'll send you the picture as soon as we hang up."

"Dad sent me an invitation to the movie premiere. I don't know if I should go, because of Caz and everything that happened." Ashley's voice dwindled at the last words.

Silence, then, "He's a total fry wipe. And he doesn't own the movie."

Knock, knock.

"Call you later." Ashley hung up.

Mom entered. She wore a big sweater and a worried look. The door clicked closed behind her.

Ashley said, "Did you see the dresses Dad sent? They're gorgeous."

Mom nodded, but her frown didn't fall away. She bit her lip and sat on the edge of Ashley's bed, clasping and unclasping her hands. Mom said, "Honey, I'd never ask you to keep something from your father."

Ashley frowned and pulled her knees toward her chest.

"It's just that maybe you could put off telling him something until I've fully worked it out?"

"Okay, sure."

Mom flattened a hand on her stomach. "You see. Well, last summer, when I visited you that weekend." Mom sucked in a breath and looked at the wall. "Well, your father and I." Her face flushed a deep red. "We love each other very much."

"I know. You're different people and can't live together."

Mom stiffened and nodded. "It's only that, sometimes, like I said, if you're not careful…" Mom's voice trailed off.

"What's wrong? I haven't heard from Dad in a week, what's going on?"

"I'm pregnant."

CHAPTER 18

"I've arranged for the limo," Marissa said to their lunch table. She offered a box of reheated fries coated with dots of red powder to the table. Everyone declined. Marissa shrugged and popped one in her mouth. "It'll pick me up, then Ashley, then Steve, then Evan." Marissa paused to wink at her boyfriend Evan. "Then we'll swing by Michelle's for photos and get everyone. Unless you want to meet me at the Fry Hut early?"

Ashley joined her friends in shaking their heads.

Marissa rooted through her bag and dug out a brochure to show them the stretch limo.

By the end of lunch, Ashley was actually excited. She welcomed the distraction from what was going on at home, and she'd probably have more fun going with her friends than a date anyway.

Michelle poked her arm with the brochure. "Tell me about your dress."

"Ice blue and long," Ashley said. "Yours?"

"Nice, you'll look like an Icee," Marissa said.

Michelle said, "Oh, Ashley, ice blue will match your eyes. How pretty. Mine's pure white, like a snow queen."

***

"Say cheese." Mom snapped another photo. "Oh, that one's so good," Mom said, examining the screen on the camera. "I'll send it to your dad." Mom's voice trailed off, and she bit her bottom lip and put a hand over her stomach. "One more."

Ashley moved over to the cinnamon-smelling Christmas candles and lifted one toward the tree. "Dry needles and fire. We need to baby-proof."

Mom waved a hand in the air. "We have months."

Mom's current philosophy was denial. If she didn't talk about the baby, they didn't have to worry about the baby or tell Dad.

The sound of tires outside meant the limo was here. Ashley's heart rate sped up and she put the candle back in its holder. Yay. Fun. She grabbed the rough edge of her crystal-beaded evening purse and tucked it under her arm.

Mom peered through the blinds, then gave Ashley a quick hug and said, "Make Marissa come in for a picture."

Ashley returned her embrace, squeezing tight for a moment, then walked down the front steps to meet her best friend. The sky was dark, but the suburban streetlights and houselights illuminated the limo clearly. The door opened, but it wasn't Marissa who got out.

It was Caz.

CHAPTER 19

She let go of her ice-blue skirt and stopped mid-sidewalk.

He waved with her notebook in his hand.

Ashley lifted her long skirt clear of the path and moved forward. The high heels made her eyes level with his mouth. He looked tired, bigger, tougher somehow. She took the small book, careful only to touch it and not Caz. "What are you doing here? Uh, you want to come in?" Her relief at having her sketches back was mixed with the confusion and rush of seeing him again.

"I came to see you. To return your notebook." His voice sounded the same—rich, deep, accented.

Ashley blinked at hearing him again in person, and turned to go up the drive, a kind of instinctual retreat in the oddness of the moment.

He said, "You look beautiful."

Ashley paused, then kept walking. "Thank you. Tonight's our winter dance." She gestured down at her dress.

Caz's hand reached up and he brushed his fingertips against her corsage. "Your date?" His British accent clipped the words.

Ashley pulled her arm away. "Uh, no. I'm going with friends."

It was so surreal to see him. Caz glowed; there was something charismatic, something over the top, about him. Even in his dark trousers and pale blue shirt, no one would mistake him for just another guy. Something marked him as more. Ashley led him into the house and gestured at the couch.

Caz sat, with straight posture, eyes on the notebook. "Olive told me you were recording notes for tabloids in it."

Ashley stiffened and sank to the cushion beside him. Answers. "And you believed her?"

"No. I don't know, I remembered how you'd never let me see it, and I wondered."

Ashley looked at him carefully: his square, tight jaw, his intense eyes.

He said, "Then I looked inside."

Her eyes widened, and she winced, feeling a flush cover her face.

"They're fascinating. Re-envisioned buildings. Idealized structures. They're not notes, so Olive lied." Caz ran a hand through his hair. "I know I could have mailed your notebook, but I wanted to see you. Talk to you."

Ashley set her purse on the couch and twisted her fingers together. It was easier to look at her French manicure than his face. "It's been months. You believe me now?"

"I want to know what happened. I want to listen." His hands opened, palms up against his knees. "I want to know about the pills that were in your bag. About the paparazzi, who were always showing up when we were alone."

Ashley knew this was a big concession for him to ask, after his parents jerked him around, his agent, his best friend. She pressed a hand to her forehead, and her crystal bracelet twinkled in the light. "You…"

Mom entered the living room with a smile of inquiry for Ashley and a greeting for Caz. "Hi, I'm Ashley's mom." Her eyes blinked and she did a double-take.

Caz rose and held out a hand. "I'm Caz." His gaze flickered to her pregnant belly, but he had the good sense not to comment.

Mom didn't act like she recognized him, though she must have. She shook his hand. "Is Marissa coming in too?"

"Uh, no," Ashley said, "Marissa's not here yet. I worked with Caz last summer." She left out the part where he got her fired. When she'd come home early, she'd just told Mom that it was because Dad had to work too much and she missed Texas. Mom hadn't questioned her.

"Oh," Mom said. "Well, why don't I get one quick photo?"

Setting her notebook beside her purse, Ashley automatically crossed over to the fireplace. As an only child, Ashley was used to the sight of her mom holding a camera and knew her duty. Her gaze flickered to Caz. She didn't know what to say, but he walked over and stood beside her, close enough that she could smell his ocean cologne, familiar, wonderful. The heaviness and warmth of his arm slid around her waist. The hard muscles of his chest pressed against her side.

Ashley held herself stiffly, trying not to lean into him, trying not to tremble. His hand squeezed her waist, and she felt the slight movement of each finger. Caz tilted his head toward hers and smiled for the photo, used to the flash. Mom offered him a drink, but he politely refused, and she left them alone.

Ashley returned to the couch and sat back. Her silk skirt fluffed around her legs, and she smoothed it with sweaty palms. "Maybe—"

"Marissa's here," Mom said from the hallway.

Ashley popped up and glanced at the clock: 6:30 p.m. Marissa, who always believed her, was waiting. Ashley took a step toward the door. "My friends are here." She grabbed her purse. The crystals bit into her palm.

Caz's warm, rough fingers encircled her wrist, halting her. Her eyes closed, and she slightly turned toward him. He said, "We need to talk and I'm scheduled to be in Los Angeles tomorrow. We're shooting a promo spot for the movie. I should really be there now."

His schedule stiffened her resolve. Ashley knew all about important Hollywood meetings. They came first. She took a step toward the door. "Sorry, I'm not letting my friends down."

"Take me with you."

His words stopped her. Ashley turned to him, eyebrows raised, eyes wide. *Take Caz to a dance at Trallwyn High School?* She didn't know how to address that astonishing proposal, so she started with the most obvious. "You're famous. The…um…well…the trailer came out."

"I've seen it." Caz rubbed his thumb against her wrist.

Ashley tried to pull her arm free, but Caz stepped closer. Ashley said, "Your appearance will cause drama, big high school drama. You'd add to it."

A horn honked from outside.

"You'd add to it big time."

Caz slid his hand to the upper part of her arm. "You can handle tabloid reporters and crazy directors. You can handle high schoolers." His voice deepened. "I have to talk to you."

The horn honked again.

"No."

"Please, we have to talk, and if you don't get me into the dance, I bet someone else at your high school will."

Ashley stepped in close and looked him in the eyes. She searched their blue-green depths for his intent, but she didn't have to look hard. Working with him all last summer told her how much he liked to get his way. He'd do it. She said, "No scene at the dance. If you go, we call a truce, and we'll talk after."

Caz nodded and clasped her hand. She tried to jerk out of his grip, but he tightened his hold. She tried to keep her fingers from trembling at the sensation of holding his hand again. He followed her back out into the lighted darkness of suburbia. Two limos were parked in front of her house. That was a first. Caz gestured toward the one in front and released her. "Let me grab my jacket."

Her fingers flexed at the loss of his, and she retreated to the second limo. Opening the door, she saw Marissa's sparkling face. Marissa snapped her tube of plum lip gloss closed, shoved it into her bag, and held up her wrist. "Check out the corsage Evan bought me. Eggplant ribbons to match my dress. He's getting the biggest kiss ever for remembering that my favorite is an orchid."

"Gorgeous." Ashley held up hers. "Mom picked white roses." The iridescent ribbons wound around the petals.

"Pretty."

Ashley moved further into the car and took a seat, leaving the door open behind her. In a rushed voice she said, "Caz showed and called a temporary truce. I'm bringing him."

Marissa's jaw dropped, and she didn't have time to close her mouth before Caz climbed in and took the seat next to Ashley, which was probably good, because it would have fallen open again when Caz grabbed Ashley's hand then smiled his movie star smile. "Hi, I'm Caz."

Marissa's mouth snapped closed and she said nothing.

Ashley totally got it. Caz was stunning in person. She hadn't let that faze her this summer, because once he became a real person to her, she just saw him as Caz, not as a famous star. Seeing him after all this time let her see him objectively. He'd put on a dark jacket. There were no other words—Caz was movie star handsome.

The limo moved forward.

Caz said, "Ashley shared one or two of your texts. They helped us get through some crazy long shoots. Did you really wear a fry costume?"

Marissa sent Ashley a mild glare then laughed. "With crazy pride. So, uh, you've gone to many of these things?"

"I was tutored on set since the age of fourteen. I've never been to a proper high school dance."

Marissa said, "Well, it'll be normal until they realize who you are."

Tensing, Ashley turned to warn Caz, "Everyone will have a cell phone."

Caz shrugged. "Probably."

Ashley looked down for a second, then held his gaze. "Okay. I want you to go with me."

***

They got out at Michelle's and her mom took photos. Together they were a group of twelve. Caz stayed in the back with her, and everyone, so absorbed in the photos, their dates, and their parents, accepted him as her date, Caz.

The twelve of them crushed into the limo built to hold ten, and Caz pulled Ashley onto his lap. She slid her arm around his neck and whispered in his ear, "You're good at the truce. Are you acting?"

Caz slid a hand to her face and put his lips to her ear to whisper, "No, this will be fun. Your friends are cool."

"They are."

He said, "If I wasn't nice, you'd probably kick me out and make me get into my own car."

"I would."

Steve pulled out a bottle of champagne. How had he hidden that from Michelle's parents?

Michelle lined up champagne flutes, Steve laced them with champagne, and Marissa topped them off with orange juice, describing the way to get perfect fresh-squeezed, and passed the glasses out.

Steve saluted their school mascot. "To the Dragons."

"Cheers."

That was when Michelle recognized Caz. She choked and stared. To Michelle's credit, she said nothing but sent a frantic look at Marissa, who nodded.

The limo jolted over another speed bump, sliding Ashley closer to Caz's chest. They were nearing the school, and it was hard to stay upright, so she relaxed against him.

Caz whispered in her ear, "Orange juice and limos."

***

Caz held her hand, and they walked up the front sidewalk surrounded by her friends, a loud, laughing group. At the entrance to the school commons, a photographer took their picture under a red balloon arch, but after that flash, they entered the gym, where the only light was provided by tiny white bulbs that twinkled.

Her friends grabbed a table in the corner, by the back wall. Ashley worried Caz would bring up their argument, but he didn't. He seemed to want to hang out. He danced, laughed, and drank the watery strawberry punch like everyone else. The evening was exhilarating, made all the better by the fact that it was too dark for anyone to recognize him. Her friends, who had by now figured out who he was, were cool enough to be quiet about his identity.

When the principal announced the King and Queen, and the cute couple took the floor, a spotlight lit up their dance and the strains of the

"Love's Romantic Ruin" ballad emerged from the speakers. Ashley sucked in a breath and stiffened. She knew the song would play tonight, it was too popular not to, but the music sounded bittersweet. Her gaze swung to Caz.

Caz stood with a quirked eyebrow and tilted chin. His hand raised, palm up. "That's *our* song." He led her to the dance floor in one of those rare perfect moments.

Head up, eyes glistening, she let him pull her into two-step position. Caz smiled wickedly then put her hand around his neck so his could slide around her waist.

Her right hand touched the back of his silky hair, and she toyed with the strands, while her left squeezed his hand. He'd disobeyed her about making a scene, but in the sweetest way possible. She closed her eyes, embracing the exquisite moment.

"Ashley, what are you doing?" The Queen said.

Caz stared at the Queen until her mouth fell open and she stopped dancing. Her partner bumped into her, and he stared at Ashley, then at Caz, then back.

The flash of a cell phone lit the dance floor. A second joined the first. A whisper reached them. More cameras flashed and the whispers got louder. That was when Ashley knew the dance had to end. She closed her eyes for a moment, leaning against his chest, wanting just one more perfect second.

Then as the song transitioned, she took his hand and said, "Run."

***

Once they settled inside the limo, Ashley tensed, and her stomach knotted. The end of the dance equaled the end of the truce. She looked out the window, upset at what was about to happen.

Caz turned her toward him. "About the —"

"Wait," Ashley said. "I want one more minute." She slipped onto his lap and put her arms around his neck. Leaning forward, she gave him a soft, sweet kiss. His mouth felt familiar, warm. Caz tasted like strawberry punch and the best parts of summer. Ashley said, "Thanks for the dance."

Caz wrapped an arm around her knees before she slipped away and he leaned into her. His right hand slid behind her head and his lips moved against hers, firm and intent.

She parted her mouth. Heaven. Rubbing his back, she resented the material that kept him from her and pushed closer. He released her mouth to draw in a shaky breath. Her brain began functioning again, and she pulled away and brushed a hand over her hair. "I —" Ashley shook her head, not really knowing what to say. Caz muttered something in French and she leaned in eagerly, hoping her additional semester of the language would help her understand him, but he didn't repeat the words.

The limo slowed in front of her house, and a flash lit the evening. The flash came from her driveway, from the large number of paparazzi standing in her yard.

Caz's face stilled and she scooted away. His expression said truce over.

Ashley looked out the tinted window, relieved the strangers couldn't see in. She'd longed to see Caz, but it had been five months, and he hadn't called once. It was so easy for him to have a fight with her and write her off, ignoring her attempts to explain like they didn't matter, like she was a liar. He'd returned for one reason: her sketchpad.

As if reading her thoughts, Caz said, "Your drawings are beautiful."

Ashley crossed her arms over her chest and felt her face flush.

"Really. The art director gave me the book. Someone had found it on the set and assumed it belonged to the art department. He said to tell you that your sketches were good. I think they're brilliant."

Ashley whispered, "You believe me now?"

"I believe you weren't writing secret notes about the cast and the set, yeah."

Her shoulders eased until more flashes came from the driveway. "And the press showing up everywhere? The pills?"

Caz shoved a hand through his hair. "You were my assistant, the only one who knew where we were going when the photographers showed up."

Her spine stiffened, and she looked at him. "That's not quite true. You knew. Maybe you wanted more media coverage." She dropped her arms and scooted forward.

Caz rolled his eyes. "That's ridiculous. Look, if your dad or the studio asked you to tip someone off, tell me. Just admit it."

"I didn't do it."

"I found the pills in your purse."

"Then someone put them there."

His whole body looked tense, as if he was fighting with himself.

"Caz, there's never going to be perfect black and white evidence or even perfect people. People screw up, but I'm telling you, I didn't do any of those things, and you have to decide right now. Either you believe me or you don't."

He stared.

"Come on, I know you've got some instincts left, dig deep. Do you believe me?"

"Yes."

Ashley sagged against the seat, not knowing why his trust mattered so much, but it did. She nodded then took hold of both of his hands and squeezed his fingers. "Good." She paused a moment, and then said, "Now, I'm ready for your apology."

"I want you to go out with me."

She shook her head and drew back. "That's not an apology."

"Ashley."

The fact that he couldn't find it in himself to apologize or even seem to recognize what he'd put her through was enough to convince Ashley that they couldn't be together. She reached for the door handle, trying to speak despite the lump in her throat. "No, trust me on this. We wouldn't work." She slipped from the car and ran through the flashing lights of the paparazzi into the house.

***

In the upcoming week, Ashley saw Caz on daytime and late night talk shows. If she missed one, her fellow students were quick to mention the interviews and ask about him. All she would say was that she and Caz had become friends over the summer when she'd been assigned as his assistant.

"Simply say you went out and broke up, no story," Marissa said.

Ashley shook her head. "Someone would put it on Facebook or Twitter. He'll know I'm talking about him." She was determined to salvage her privacy, plus she didn't want to look back. She wanted to move on.

CHAPTER 20

Ashley tugged her bag off the carousel at LAX, careful not to let the garment bag she'd carried on hit the linoleum. It held the three designer dresses Dad had sent, and she wanted to send pictures to Powder so she'd wear the right one to the movie premiere.

"Hey, kiddo," Dad said.

She turned in surprise, and found Dad standing behind her with pink roses in his hand. He held an arm out for a hug.

***

Excitement warred with anxiety as her dad escorted her down the red carpet on premiere night of *Eternal Loss, Eternal Revenge*. They showed their credentials to security and were shown inside the roped-off area that led into the theater.

Dad eyed some other suit-wearers. "I see Russ. I need to talk to him for a second. Want to join me so I can show off my gorgeous daughter?"

Ashley froze. Russ. That was the director. She'd never told Dad about getting fired, and in the back of her mind, she had a real fear that she'd be escorted away from the premiere as soon as an executive spotted her. She turned, keeping her back to the director, and said, "No, thanks. I'll see you inside." She tried to keep the squeak from her voice.

"Have fun." Dad patted her shoulder and headed toward the men.

Ashley swallowed and moved further in. The electric crowd of screaming fans with their flashing cameras was contained by ropes and strategically placed security guards. She snapped their photo from this side of the ropes and forwarded the picture to Mom and Marissa.

A ton of movie stars not attached to the film came to the premiere.

While it was fun to see them, Ashley wasn't starstruck. She'd really met too many actors growing up who'd come and gone in popularity to feel awe.

"Ashley!"

Ashley turned.

"Hey girl." Powder stood with her arms out. She looked rock-star in a black and silver gown. Her hair had grown several inches but was still spiked out.

Ashley hugged her, and her own dress—white and filmy—swirled around them with the motion and the faint California breeze. "Thanks for helping me choose a dress."

"Your dad knows some killer designers. And you look perfect, very springtime."

"Thanks." Ashley admired Powder's style. She'd never be able to carry off metal studs. "You look so cool."

Powder smiled her thanks then eyed the growing crowd of arriving stars. "I can't leave Jason or some starlet will make a play at him. Find me later, okay?"

Ashley nodded. On her way up the carpet, she ran into several other people she'd worked with, and they chatted about the crowd and expectations for the film. If they knew she'd gotten fired, no one brought it up, so Ashley relaxed and began to enjoy herself more. No doubt her minor set drama was nothing compared to what they saw every day at work. And during one of her August texts, Powder had said Ashley's departure had been glossed over.

Ashley knew more people than she thought she would and welcomed seeing most of them. Boomer's sheer size made him easy to spot, but she almost didn't recognize him in sleeves. She hugged him and complimented his suit. "Powder told me you got a part in Petra's next film."

Boomer looked down and she'd have sworn he blushed. "They came to sign her, and I was doing some sound work nearby. They thought I'd be good for a small part."

"You'll be great."

Boomer grinned and cocked his head, back to his normal, confident self. "That's because I'll be traveling with the side arms." He curled his biceps for her. "Loaded with bullets."

"Okay, yeah, see ya later." Ashley patted him on his impressive bicep, and moved a few steps down the red carpet. Halfway down, she ran into the director.

She stopped and her face flushed. They last time they'd been face-to-face, he'd fired her from the film.

Nothing showed on his face but welcome. He pulled away from the couple he was speaking with and leaned down to hug her. "Hi. What do you think of all this?"

Ashley breathed out a sigh of relief. Good. No trouble. She said truthfully, "It's exciting."

"A lot of what you did really worked and we used it."

"Cool."

"See you inside."

Ashley took that as her cue to leave. She walked along toward the building, glad they'd come early so she had a chance to catch up with people. This was turning out better than okay.

Up ahead stood Cutter, hair coiffed in a perfect swoop, wearing a shiny purple suit with trousers cuffed high over brown loafers. Cutter reached out a hand and grabbed her arm. His eyes looked glittery and they shifted around the crowd. He leaned close. "He's here, have you seen him?" His voice sounded thin, strained.

Her heart thumped. "Who?"

Cutter's hand tightened against her arm until it hurt, and his face flushed. "Harlon Ramonannini."

Ashley shook loose. "No."

"Yes!" Cutter moaned. "He's going to see. He's going to know I recut his wedding dress." He crossed his arms over his chest.

Ah. Ashley realized the reason for Cutter's panic—the bridal gown flounce alteration. "You made the dress drape better." She gentled her tone to reassure him.

Desperation flashed in his eyes, and Cutter's voice took on a hysterical edge. "You know nothing," he said and dashed away.

If the yells of the fans were any indication, more stars had arrived. Things were heating up on the red carpet, so she knew it was time to make her way inside. She wanted to see Caz more than anything, but she also didn't want to see him. Maybe she'd catch him inside, and they'd share a quiet, civil moment away from the commotion. Dad had said the movie premiere's auditorium sat about a thousand people. In that large a crowd, she may not even see the back of his head. Had Caz brought a date? Would he—?

Her thoughts were interrupted by a hand on her arm and a heavy accent. "Score."

"Excuse me?" Ashley pulled free of Garrett's hold.

"I told Caz I'd find you." Garrett tilted his head at a confident angle. His shorter hair stopped inches from the collar of his tuxedo jacket. Under it, he wore an off-white shirt untucked over his blue kilt. "He's looking all over the place for you."

"You're talking to Caz?"

Garrett grinned big. "Yeah, we're great mates again." He threw an arm around her shoulders, keeping her in place, close enough that the wool fabric of his kilt brushed her fingers. "Caz called in his marker and I'm about to deliver." Using the pressure of his big arm against her shoulders, Garrett turned her back into the crowd.

They'd made up? Good. Ashley tried to duck under his heavy arm. "I'm just going inside."

His arm didn't budge. "Nope, I owe him, and there he is." Garrett pointed with his free hand. Ashley saw a dark-suited Caz shaking hands and signing autographs with the fans behind the rope. He looked wonderful, his hair slightly longer, streaked. A security guard with an earpiece flanked him, and his thin agent, dressed in a dark pantsuit, trailed close by.

Garrett forced her straight toward Caz with no intention of stopping. "Come on, then, before he goes mental."

Ashley stumbled in her tall, strappy heels. "Slow down. He's working, we can't—"

Garrett lowered his arm to her waist, ignored her protests, and propelled her forward until she stood within a foot of Caz.

Shouts of "Caspian" came from the crowd. It was deafening, like the day they'd first met, but even louder.

"Here she is, mate." Garrett clamped a hand on Caz's shoulder. His arm dropped from her waist.

Caz turned at the touch and faced her.

Caz. Here. Now. A shock went through her body and the noise dulled.

His blue-green eyes searched hers.

"I'll leave you to it, then," Garrett said. "I want to do my duty and get inside before all the finger foods disappear. I hear they have puff pastries with crab and capers." He swaggered toward the roped-off fans.

A bright light hit her eyes and she blinked against the white spots, shaken out of her trance. She dug in her purse for her sunglasses and shoved them on. The camera flashes had intensified now that she was this close to Caz. This was too much. It was time to head for the entrance.

Caz stepped close and grabbed her hand. Her nerves tightened. The crowd continued its chanting roar. "Caspian!"

Ashley quickly pulled free of his grip.

"Wait."

Ashley couldn't really hear the word but she read it on his lips. "Inside," she said. "I'll see you inside."

His agent gestured toward a dais set up for interviews.

Caz shook his head at her. "Just a minute."

Ashley looked over her shoulder toward the premiere entrance.

Caz put his mouth against her ear and kind of yelled, "Please wait. I'm talking to Garrett, did you see?"

Be gracious and distant, she told herself. Stay out of his personal life. She'd practiced the words at home and on the plane a number of times. She was going to say that he looked great and wish him luck on the film. Putting her mouth to his ear, Ashley said instead, "I'm glad." She breathed in the fragrance of his ocean shower gel, and calmed. "No, sorry, um, I meant good luck on the film. It's good to see you again. I'll catch you later."

His agent moved in. "You're scheduled to—"

"A minute," Caz said urgently.

His agent touched Caz's elbow. "She can stay with us, but we have to move forward."

Caz shook his head and folded his arm, staying put.

His agent turned to Ashley. "Nice to see you again, Ashley, but you're causing a delay." Her tone didn't sound like it was nice to see her again. She glanced up ahead. "We have to move."

Caz's lips tightened.

Familiar with Caz's stubborn streak, Ashley nodded. She motioned toward the agent, indicating she should lead. "Which way?"

Caz clenched his hands and followed them. Two paces in, he unclenched one and reached for her hand. Ashley stayed out of his reach. Mixed feelings swamped her. He moved closer until they reached the steps that led up to a platform.

Petra stood on top, being interviewed. She wore a fuchsia-colored dress, and a matching, jeweled hairclip that held back half of her dark hair. Swiveling her hips, she swept her train into one hand and held the skirts toward the reporter. If looks were anything to go by, the interviewer was getting a rundown about each thread.

An assistant wearing an earpiece held up a hand in Caz's direction.

"Promise me you'll wait," Caz said.

Ashley looked around. A lot of people were headed for the auditorium. "Um."

"You have to promise me, or I walk out, and leave with you now."

Sometimes he could be very British and understated. That was how he gave the illusion that he was normal—not tonight though. He'd had weeks to call her, and he wanted to talk while they were on the red carpet with a million eyes and cameras on them.

"Promise me," Caz said.

"I promise."

Caz lifted her sunglasses to look in her eyes.

"I promise. Go."

He put a warm hand to the side of her face and whispered in her ear. "I hoped you'd be here."

"They're ready for you, Mr. Thaymore."

Caz's fingers slowly fell from Ashley's cheek. He gave her sunglasses back and jogged up the steps to join Petra and the interviewer.

Petra hooked her arm through his.

The crowd chanted, "CasPet, CasPet." Petra waved to the crowd in response. Caz didn't turn. He faced the reporter and spoke into a microphone, and it was only a few minutes before he jogged back down to her. Petra remained on the platform, still talking.

Caz took her hand. "Okay, then, let's get inside."

Ashley tugged against his hold, but he wouldn't release her. The more the cameras flashed, the more she pulled, a smile pasted on her lips to keep up impressions. Realizing he wasn't going to let go, Ashley stopped the struggle and said through her smile, "What are you doing?" She hoped he heard her over the crowd.

Caz leaned closer and tilted his head. "I can demonstrate better if you want."

Her heart thumped and Ashley jerked quickly back. "No. Inside."

Someone pushed in from behind her, propelling her into Caz's hard body. Caz stopped her fall and put his arm around her waist.

"Excuse me." The redheaded Lorene pushed past them dressed in a green hoop-skirted dress, à la Scarlett O'Hara, and climbed the steps. When she reached the top, she put her hands on her hips.

Petra finished answering her interview question before facing Lorene.

Lorene shouted, "You stole my part." The words were loud enough that anyone below the dais could hear.

Petra touched her fingertips to her chest, in a *who me* gesture. Lorene narrowed in.

The security guard left Caz's side and took the steps two at a time. Lorene pushed Petra. Petra hit the rail and the metal framework shook. After pausing in a carefully draped pose, Petra lunged forward and shoved back. The camera moved in for a close-up.

"The bikini ski instructor gig was mine," Lorene said.

Petra formed her hands around imaginary skis and pushed off. Lorene screamed. The suited security guard grabbed her and dragged her wriggling, protesting body out of view.

Petra put a limp hand on her forehead and glided back to the interviewer, leaning into the microphone.

Caz's agent rushed forward. "Go up there. See if Petra's okay."

"She's fine," Caz said.

"You're co-stars. Go." His agent took out a cigarette.

Caz shook his head.

"You owe it to the film."

Caz stiffened and his fingers tightened against Ashley's fingers. "The film is complete. The interviews are complete. My owing them anything is over."

The agent dug for her lighter. She didn't light the cigarette, but she tapped the end against the top of the lighter. "Ashley, you don't mind waiting, do you? I need to speak to Caspian about this opportunity."

"I—" Ashley didn't get to finish her sentence before Caz got between her and the agent.

"You're fired."

His agent narrowed her eyes and lit her cigarette, but she didn't say anything, just sucked in a deep draw of the cigarette and exhaled the acrid smoke.

Caz said nothing more. He turned to the entrance of the theater, leading Ashley by the hand. Numerous people tried to stop him for a chat, but Caz made them walk and talk because he didn't pause for anyone. Inside, the lobby was almost as loud, with everyone excited to see the film.

Ashley took off her sunglasses. Fired. He'd just fired his agent. She'd thought he should do that ever since the photo shoot, but now the word made her stomach clench.

"When we were in the car, in front of your house in Houston, I knew," Caz said.

"You just fired your agent."

Caz rolled his shoulders. "Yeah." His eyes looked out to the horizon before turning back to her. "I should have followed you into your house."

They were having two different conversations.

A studio executive pushed his way between them to shake Caz's hand. "Looking forward to the film."

"Thanks," Caz said, and the man moved on.

The AD interrupted them next. He'd trimmed his goatee short and looked as tense as he'd looked on set. After shaking Caz's hand, he offered a handshake to Ashley. She shook awkwardly with her left hand because Caz still refused to relinquish her right.

The AD said, "Evening. You two excited to see the final cut?"

"Absolutely," Ashley said.

Caz gave a small nod.

"Great," the AD said. "You're going to love it."

A woman wearing a suit joined them, saying something about high pre-sale ticket records. The greetings weren't going to stop coming. The premiere was an impossible place for a private conversation.

Caz headed from the lobby to the entrance of the auditorium. "Caspian Thaymore, plus one," he said to the usher. The usher grinned and led them inside. The theater was a large typical stadium-style movie theater. The air even had that faint, popcorn-lives-here smell. The bright wall sconces lit the darkness so people could find their seats. After getting a quick autograph from Caz, the usher pointed them to the middle section.

"Thanks."

Caz put his hand on the small of her back, propelling her down the row. "I went by your house earlier, hoping you'd be in town for the premiere, but you weren't, and your dad wouldn't give me any details."

Ashley sank into her seat. "He's protective."

"I missed you," Caz said, keeping his voice low as he lowered beside her. "I know I screwed up."

He had. Ashley closed her eyes a second. So had everyone around him. "I get it. I do. So many people used you all summer, in so many ways. That's your life. How could you not, how could you—"

Caz cut her off with his kiss. It felt familiar, exciting. His kiss had the power to shut off her thoughts and it ended too fast.

Pulling back, he laid his free hand against her face. "I wanted to call for Christmas, but I didn't, and things were crap at home. My dad came back with false apologies, and he's already left again."

"Are you mad at him for leaving, or your mom for taking him back?"

"Both."

"Did you find out who did the press leaks?"

"Petra and my driver. My agent too."

She gaped at him. "All of them?"

"It's why it never made sense before, because it was all these random locations, and you were the only one who knew them all."

Ashley looked away. "How do you stand Hollywood? How can you work with these people again?"

"Petra has her own agenda, but she's not malicious." His expression was hard. "I'm hiring my own driver and buying a car."

"And the pills?"

"I don't know who drugged my drink, but I know it wasn't you."

"It wasn't."

Looking into her eyes with a sincere expression, Caz said, "I know. I'm sorry I doubted you before." He kissed her, a brief, quick kiss. "I know words don't mean much, but I'm truly sorry about what happened."

Her lips tingled and the feeling contrasted with the emotional rush. He believed her.

People filtered into the theater ending their private conversation. Many stopped to offer comments and congratulations to Caz. The noise level grew until the director moved to the floor in front of the screen. He leaned into the rail and spoke into a microphone. “Thank you all for coming. This project has been a labor of love for the cast and crew, without whom we wouldn’t be here tonight. So without further adieu, enjoy the film.”

The lights darkened and Ashley felt her lips smile. She squeezed Caz’s hand.

The movie came on.

OMG.

Halfway through the movie, Ashley dropped Caz’s hand and wrapped her arms around herself. The director had used all of her scenes, and he replayed the steamy bed scene the most. He replayed them throughout the film. Images of her in bed with Caz flashed through the hero’s mind repeatedly. The death scene showed too, but the bed scene definitely made the most appearances.

Ashley rubbed a hand over her face, half covering her eyes until it ended and the credits rolled.

Leaving the auditorium, in between chats with people stopping them, Caz said, “Why are you so upset?”

Ashley turned her face to him and whispered, “He shot when I didn’t even know he was rolling.”

“Well, that’s not a bad way to get a natural take.”

“And the bed. We’re rolling around on that bed. A really long time. He put that in the film.” She didn’t think her face could flush any deeper.

“You looked hot. You’re beautiful, Ashley.”

“My dad is in the audience.” Her voice raised on the last word.

Caz sucked in a breath. “Ah, maybe too hot then.”

Ashley turned her face into his arm with a groan. “Yes, definitely too hot.”

His hand rubbed her back. “It was a good film, though, right? I don’t always get to say that.”

She didn’t answer and didn’t explain the part that shocked her the most. The depth of the emotions she’d seen on screen didn’t come from any hidden talent. She wasn’t an actor. As much as she lied to herself, she had just seen her feelings for him, right there, in high definition. She was in love with Caspian Thaymore.

In somewhat of a daze, she exited the theater along the side of the auditorium. The red carpet was still out, but the roped-off fan area had cleared.

Powder appeared and hugged Ashley. "You were so good."

Ashley got out of her own head. "Thanks. Your makeup was stunning. I admit I didn't fully appreciate your art until your work was blown up on screen."

Powder laughed. "Yep, there's nothing better than seventy feet of screen to highlight your mistakes."

Petra, Cutter, and the wave of their clashing colognes joined them. Olive, arms swinging, arrived soon after. Olive wore an all-black gown and low-heeled shoes. She carried a large leather tote.

Cutter did a small jig and the tassels on his shoes shook. "He saw it. He loved it."

"Harlon?"

Cutter's voice took on a singsong tone and his face held a glow. "Harlon Ramonannini saw my revision and loved it."

"Cool."

Petra did one of her poses from the movie. "My wardrobe was fantastic too. Did you see how great I looked? In every scene, it was amazing."

Olive nodded. "Amazing."

"It was so intense," Petra said. "I was so keyed up last night I could barely sleep. I really don't know how I kept from looking hideous tonight. I had to put on so much eye makeup because of the shadows." She blinked at Powder who gave her a thumbs up.

Caz pulled Ashley in front of him and draped his arms around her. She leaned against him.

Cutter eyed their embrace with surprise. "Ashley, I thought you were dating Garrett."

"I never went out with Garrett."

"That's what I thought, but Olive was so insistent." Cutter put his hands on his hips and pouted at Olive. "Guess your source isn't as good as you thought."

Petra waved her arms in a dismissive gesture. "Olive is a great assistant, but her scoop is always off. Mine, however, is great. I mean, when I see something I get the story right. Like with Lorene, I knew she was drinking, and I told everyone how she is on a set. But Olive was like 'Poor Lorene must have been drugged.' Please. I know Lorene, I've worked with her, so I know. I was all like 'I don't think so' and Olive was like *no really*. You remember that, Olive, right? How wrong you were and how I was right?"

Olive shifted her eyes from left to right then looked up. "I don't know who said that, but you're right, she was drinking."

"I know," Petra said. "You should listen to me. Lorene and I are frenemies. I was telling *Tween In*, I'm in the know."

Caz's arms tensed against Ashley. "What a stupid misunderstanding," he whispered in her ear.

Ashley turned her gaze up to his, and his ocean eyes pleaded with her. She put her hand over his and squeezed.

Over Caz's shoulder, a group of well-dressed executives shifted. Dad stood dead center in their midst, wearing a dark frown. His gaze met hers and he strode over.

Ashley swallowed and ducked out from under Caz's embrace, stepping away.

Dad took her arm and pulled her back another step. He wore a polite smile but his icy eyes held fury as he addressed her small circle. "If you'll excuse me, I need to speak to my daughter."

Olive gasped. "Ashley is your daughter?" She looked at Ashley. "Why didn't you tell us your dad was Mr. Herrington?" Her gaze swung back to Ashley's dad. "I was just telling Ashley how great she was."

"Hurry back, Ashley," Petra said. "So we can catch up. I have some notes I can give you on your performance. I've been doing this a long time and can help you out."

Cutter said, "We've got to get together again soon."

Dad barely gave them a nod. He cupped her elbow in an unshakable grip and walked toward the side of the building. His low voice came out slow and angry. "What the hell were you doing all summer?"

Caz followed them, his arms across his chest.

Dad barely spared him a glance. "You need to get back to your promoting."

Caz said, "I can give Ashley a lift home. We can talk about this there."

Dad's eyebrows rose, and his voice thinned. "Stay out of it."

Ashley stepped between them, trying to calm things down. "I just helped out when Lorene didn't show up. I wore a wig. You can't even really tell it was me." Her voice dwindled on the last words. She didn't believe them so it was hard to sell them.

"Really?" Dad said. "You think so? You think the kids in your high school won't find out? You think a guy is going to treat you with respect, after seeing that? That bed scene?"

Caz stepped close. "She was acting. We hadn't been dating that long when we shot that."

Ashley widened her eyes and shook her head at Caz. Now was not the time to go there.

"Dating?" Dad turned to Ashley. "*Are you kidding me? He's an actor*.

He's not even in school. What are you thinking?"

Caz's eyes glittered under his frown. "Didn't you know?""

Dad looked confused and annoyed. "This is because I don't live with you, isn't it? Boys wouldn't try that crap if I spent more time home with you and your mom."

Ashley's eyes widened, and she was knocked so far off her foundation, she didn't know what to say.

The director joined them, so Dad redirected his anger, and whatever else he was about to say was replaced with, "What the hell, Russ?"

The director held up his hands. "Now, I know, I know, we ended up using a lot of her work in the finished film. But you've got admit the shots look great."

"My daughter's going to be an architect. Not an actress. An architect. I arranged for her to work with the set designers and said she could help with other tasks as needed. As needed, Russ, I didn't say shit about her being on film." Dad jabbed a hand toward the movie poster.

Ashley's shoulders relaxed. "Really?" That made so much more sense in regards to Dad going on and on about this helping with her college applications. He'd arranged for her to work with the architect. That was thoughtful. "I would have loved to work with the architect."

That seemed to make Dad angrier. "Then why didn't you tell me you weren't?"

She hadn't known she was supposed to be working with an architect so why would she have told him she wasn't? She shrugged. "I didn't see you that much."

Dad pressed his lips together, then said, "I started dating an actress, Bevan, in July, and I know how you feel about the stupidity of dating actors, so maybe I stayed away a bit too much."

The director glanced around at the lingering crowd. "Where is Bevan tonight?"

Dad glared.

The director held up a hand. "There is the media coverage. She'd like it. Also, this is a great story for Ashley. How Ashley stepped up to help out and—"

Dad's lips all but disappeared and his jaw tensed. He jabbed a finger in a different direction, and the director followed. As they walked away, Dad said, "You're not mentioning Ashley to the press."

"They're here now," the director said. "The cameras are on us now."

"Not one word."

Their conversation lowered until Ashley could no longer hear them, but the head shaking and body stance looked adversarial.

The ground trembled.

CHAPTER 21

Ashley didn't react other than to stay still. She felt like a true Californian in that moment. Earthquake? Who worries about earthquakes?

Movie posters swayed on the wall of the theater, and she lost her insouciance.

"Earthquake!" someone shouted. Several people screamed. Cutter's shriek pierced the night. Ashley turned toward him and saw the large temporary platform sway. Weird. Only a few hours ago, Caz had been standing on top giving an interview. One of its large corner metal poles bent as if it were made of something other than steel.

Caz grabbed her and yanked her away from the falling structure.

The horrible sound of crashing metal and the sharp crack of splintering wood filled the air. Screams got louder. She tried to lift her head, but could only see Caz on top of her.

He said, "Are you okay?"

Wriggling, she eased from beneath his weight and pulled herself into a seated position with her back against the exterior brick wall of the auditorium. On the other side of Caz, half the fallen platform squatted like a crumpled metal spider, and half balanced against the side of the auditorium, trapping them in a debris cocoon. Pieces of the metal structure had ripped through banners advertising the premiere, and other pieces broke off, clanging through the night. Caz had thrown her clear just as the structure fell. She quickly looked him over, noting dust in his hair and tears on the sleeves of his jacket.

"Are you okay?" she asked, her heart pounding.

"Just a normal evening for me." Caz struggled to sit up beside her. The space was a tighter fit for him. The outer framework formed a small haven amid the debris.

He had the British ability to underplay situations when he wanted to use it. Ashley put a hand over her heart to feel its beat ease and put a tense hand on his arm. Caz pulled her close and she curled onto his lap.

He rubbed a hand across her back. "We can crawl out through there."

Her gaze followed his fingers. There was a significant gap between the platform and the ground.

Yells and sirens sounded, adding their noise as a backdrop to the slide of additional debris and indistinguishable yells from the event-goers. Ashley turned toward the rubble as a terrible thought hit her, and she screamed, "Dad!" She tried to rise.

Caz's hand pulled her back down. "Don't scream. There's dust. Your dad wasn't near us. He's okay." He brushed a hand over her arm and pointed toward the crawl space. "Let's go through."

"We can't. The architect told me about that." Ashley tried to keep the panic out of her voice. "You can't build permanent things with that metal here in California because it won't withstand earthquakes. There could be aftershocks."

Caz looked ready to argue, but her tense grip and whatever was in her eyes made him agree.

There wasn't room in their nook for her to stand. The sensation of being trapped and the creaking of the metal around her made her heart pound and her pulse race. "It's going to fall again. We're stuck. I can't see my dad." She peered through the darkness. "Dad!" she screamed again.

Caz pulled a cell phone from his jacket. "Try him."

Ashley tapped in his number with shaking fingers. A busy signal beeped on the other end. She hit the end key and typed again. This time she pinged a text and sent an email.

Beep.

The response was immediate. Dad's response read, "Hold tight. Fire crew on it. All okay here."

She slumped against Caz. His hand covered hers and he read the message over her shoulder. She buried her face against his neck, trying to stop trembling.

"When you're an architect you could construct us a better platform."

Her arms tightened on his shoulders. "Okay."

Crash. The small tunnel he'd suggested they crawl through collapsed completely, stirring up more dirt and debris. They lowered their faces away from the projectiles and pluming dust.

His arms tightened around her. "Good call."

"I hope everyone's okay."

"Me too." Caz stroked her hair. He sent a few texts out and shared the replies with her. "Garrett's gone to the pub. He'll hold us a seat."

Ashley melted deeper into him and they clung together a long time, not talking until her jumbled thoughts turned to their fight; not that any of it mattered now, but the thoughts ate at her. She looked into his eyes. "May I ask you something?"

"Anything."

"How can you be so friendly with people you know used you or tried to, like some of these people from the studio? But when it was Garrett and me, you wrote us off."

His hand stilled against her face. "I don't give a toss about the others."

Ashley toyed with his hand, her fingers trembling.

His hand slid into her hair, and his voice took on a serious tone. "I'll believe you next time. Always. I swear."

While they waited for the rescue crew Ashley told him about seeing Olive with the pill bottle and overhearing Olive talk to Petra about pregnancy that first day on set.

Caz didn't take away what she thought he would from her story. He looked disappointed and said, "So you didn't fancy me? The box wasn't an invitation?"

"I was saving you from a lifetime of being someone's baby-daddy. You should be thankful."

Caz shook his head. "No. I was hoping you fancied me."

"I fancy you now." Ashley brushed at some of the dirt on his sleeve. "Well, I do when you're not so dirty." She looked directly into his eyes. "Thanks for saving me from the earthquake."

He brushed a strand of hair off her cheek. "Maybe your dad will let you date me now."

"Probably not."

"Yes."

"Then I could really show you how to kiss."

He smiled.

Hands broke through the rubble. "Caspian, give us your hands."

Caz pushed her forward. "Get my girlfriend out first."

Ashley tried to stay as still as possible while they pulled her free, worried about knocking more rubble down onto Caz. The metal creaked and dust flew up. Arms lifted her and passed her across the heap to a firefighter on the edge of the rubble. He lowered her down on the pavement. Ashley turned back to wait for Caz.

Another firefighter appeared at her right elbow. She placed an oxygen mask over Ashley's face and pulled her arm. "You have to get out of their way and let them work." The firefighter led her over to an ambulance and a paramedic checked her out.

Dad ran through the crowd and grabbed her in a hug.

Ashley pulled the oxygen mask off. "I'm okay."

He pushed the mask back in place. "We'll see what the doctor says." Another firefighter walked up with Caz, pointing at the ambulance.

Caz, covered in dust, coughed and shook his head. "I'm fine."

Ashley grabbed him in a hug.

"You're going," Dad said to Ashley. He looked at Caz. "He can stay if he wants. The press probably wants to talk to him."

Caz frowned, and coughed into his arm. "I'm going with Ashley." The paramedic put an oxygen mask over his face and Caz shrugged out of his dirty jacket.

"I can take care of my daughter." Dad brushed a hand against her hair. "We need to call your mom before she sees this on the news."

Caz lifted his mask and said, "Yeah, the stress can't be good for someone that pregnant."

Ashley shook her head and wiped her hand across her neck, her eyes frantically telling Caz to stop talking.

"What?" Dad said. "Pregnant?"

Ashley kept her mask on and avoided his gaze.

Dad lifted the mask away enough so she could speak. Her words came out fast, between coughs. "Mom's going to tell you. But she knows you're busy, and didn't want to burden you. You know Mom."

He put the mask back in place. "Burden me?" His voice tensed and all his calm strength left as he said, "She's pregnant? Why the secrecy?" His tone held a combination of shock, outrage, and concern. "Is your mom okay?"

Ashley held both thumbs up.

Dad looked incredulous. "Why am I the last to know?"

"You didn't bother to see Ashley all summer," Caz said.

Ashley shook her head at Caz again and tried to put the oxygen over his mouth.

"That's one of the reasons it's stupid to date an actor. Their priorities aren't straight. That's why I dumped Bevan." Dad faced her and put his hands on her arms. "Nothing is more important than my kid."

Ashley returned his hug and adjusted her mask to whisper, "Kids."

Dad stiffened.

EPILOGUE

Ashley stood with her back against the column at Royce Hall with her UCLA campus classmates. She felt too giddy at having completed finals to go through the usual post-exam second-guessing. Her fall freshman quarter was complete. She tilted her head back, smiled at the arch above them then at her friends, and powered her phone back on. The indicator flashed four text messages.

Dad: "How'd your English lit final go?"

Click. "Are you done? Are you exhausted? Spaghetti tonight, love, Mom."

Click. "You better not be wearing sweats. I don't care if it is finals, Powder."

She was, navy ones, and her hair was pulled into a ponytail. Powder would die.

Click. Marissa: "Pastry final done. Aced it. Yay. You?"

"Going out with us to celebrate?" One of the guys asked and stepped closer.

Ashley shook her head.

Another classmate said, "Let me guess, your boyfriend is out of town for work again?"

One of the girls rolled her eyes. "You know she only says she has a boyfriend so you'll stop hounding her to go out with you."

A Bentley Continental Supersports convertible pulled up, and her boyfriend got out. Wearing dark Oakley sunglasses and walking with a movie star swagger, Caz headed straight up the path toward them.

Ashley grinned and a surge of emotion rushed through her. She missed him when he went on location.

Caz's arm went around her, and he shouldered her backpack before kissing her in a fast *hello* kiss. "Hiya."

"Hi." Ashley relaxed against him then introduced her friends.

Caz overlooked their dropped jaws and said, "Hi."

After the greetings, she and Caz walked hand in hand toward his new car. His blue green eyes met hers. "I missed you. My assistant on set did not compare."

Ashley laughed. "That's good." She hugged him and breathed in. "I missed your cologne. Next time, I'll visit more on the weekends."

Caz's smile had her favorite wicked edge. "Yes."

"Did you get your UCLA registration complete?"

"Yeah. And we have three weeks off until the next quarter starts. I can't remember the last time I had three weeks off."

Ashley squeezed his hand. "You'll love it."

Caz scanned the campus. "One term on, and one off. Your baby brother will be in college before I finish my bachelor's."

"You are so looking forward to it."

"Yeah. And maybe your dad will ease up, now that I'm a student."

"Maybe. Mom and Dad want us to come to dinner. I try and eat there as much as possible to ease Mom into her new California lifestyle. Dad's trying too."

"Your Mom and Dad want me to come over?"

"Mom does."

Caz nodded. They neared the ice-blue car.

Ashley's eyebrows raised. "Nice car."

"I picked the color, but the car was a bonus from the studio."

"Huh, I'm not sure I received a gift for all my work as a PA."

Caz opened her car door and kissed away her smirk. "You got me."

Other Books By Emily Evans:

The Prince with Amnesia

The Boarding School Experiment

Do Over

The Kissing Deadline

Epic Escape

Made in the USA
Columbia, SC
23 May 2023